WILD MAN OF THE WOODS

Joan Clark

VIKING KESTREL

VIKING KESTREL

Penguin Books Canada Ltd., 2801 John Street,
Markham, Ontario, Canada L3R 1B4

Penguin Books, Harmondsworth, Middlesex,
England

Viking Penguin Inc., 40 West 23rd Street, New York
U.S.A.

Penguin Books Australia Ltd., Ringwood, Victoria,
Australia

Penguin Books (N.Z.) Ltd., Private Bag, Takapuna
Auckland 9, New Zealand

First published by Penguin Books Canada Ltd., 1985

Printed in the United States of America

Canadian Cataloguing in Publication Data

Clark, Joan, 1934-
 Wild man of the woods

ISBN 0-670-80015-5

I. Title

PS8555.L353W55 1985   jC813'.54   C85-098645-1
PZ7.C53Wi 1985

For Tim and Tony

WILD MAN
OF THE WOODS

One

Stephen's face pressed close to the window as the bus sped past mountains lying like sleeping dinosaurs beneath a summer moon. In the dark gaps between peaks he imagined deep forests, canyons, caves, mysteries forever beyond his reach. This was Stephen's first trip on a Greyhound: he was used to city buses, short jaunts past skyscrapers shining with glassy boldness in bright sunlight.

He had left the city in mid-afternoon and ever since had been speeding westward towards mountains, probing deeper and deeper into their massive flanks so that now, several hundred miles later, he found himself surrounded by mountains.

The bus began to climb a long, winding hill.

Stephen watched lights come flickering into view, lights distant and singular as stars. By the time the bus had reached the plateau where the village was, the light seemed like soldiers' campfires, burning bright and close together.

The village was his destination. The bus pulled up in front of a general food store. Stephen stared into the grey dark searching for his cousin Louie. There was no sign of him. Stephen swallowed against a thickening in his throat. What if the Barrows forgot he was arriving this evening? What if he was stranded outside this store all night? What if . . . ?

But no, the Barrows couldn't forget, because this was an exchange visit. This afternoon, as he had been boarding the bus in the city to come here, his cousin Mad had been boarding a bus here to travel there. At this moment she would be staring out the bus window in the Greyhound depot, searching for his sister Selena. Mad's bus must have glided past his on the road somewhere in the mountains. He hadn't seen it; probably it had slipped past when he'd been looking the other way.

The passengers were lifting down bags from overhead racks. Stephen got up and took down his new knapsack bought especially for this trip: he was looking forward to going on hikes and campouts with Louie during the month. The knapsack was equipped with metal plates and cups, water canteen, jack-knife, rope, matches and insect repellent. There was also a heavy book entitled *Great Masks* inside his knapsack. It was a gift from his parents for his aunt and uncle.

Passengers were getting off, so Stephen walked up the aisle and waited his turn, half wanting to stay on the bus in case the Barrows weren't there. But soon he was stepping down, and there was Aunt Lise, crushing his head against her sweater, which smelled of wood-smoke. If his mother had done this, Stephen would have been embarrassed, but now he was glad of a hug. There was Uncle Adam with his bulky paunch and big grin riffling his hair and asking how he was.

"Hi." Louie stood shyly behind his parents, hands in his pockets, watching Stephen. Profiled against the store window, half of Louie's face was alien pale, the other half hidden in darkness.

"Hi," Stephen said.

Neither boy moved.

Then Uncle Adam took his knapsack. Aunt Lise asked him how many bags he had. Louie turned into the full light of the window and smiled. And in this dark-eyed, dark-haired stranger Stephen caught his first glimpse of the cousin he remembered from the last time he'd seen him, three years ago.

They got the bags out of the storage compartment in the bus's underbelly. The bags were battered — Stephen's father had taken the good bags with him to Greece — but in the dark nobody noticed. Anyway, Uncle Adam wasn't rich enough to care. Once his uncle had been rich, but that was years ago, before he'd had a heart attack and given up dentistry to become a wood carver. Aunt Lise had given up nursing to become a weaver. They had spent their savings buying land and building a log house with a studio in it. Selling their carvings and weavings was how they made their money now, but it wasn't much.

Uncle Adam swung the bags into the back of a badly dented red pickup. Louie climbed up and sat on a blanket, his back against the cab. Stephen climbed up after him. He had never ridden in the back of a truck before. Aunt Lise got in the cab beside Uncle Adam and they were off, the truck rattling over the gravel, then onto pavement. Soon they were driving away from the village. The campfire lights dwindled, becoming as sporadic as starlight, difficult to distinguish from real stars. The narrow road plunged into a valley night-thick with trees.

Stephen hugged his jacket closer. The air was cool, much cooler than in the city. Beside him he felt Louie's shoulder brush his as the truck jolted over bumps. The road began to climb upward, curving around the base of a mountain, the moon bathing the landscape in a phosphorescent sheen. Stephen glanced sideways at Louie's face, sharply chiselled by the light.

Louie turned. "Listen," he said.

From far to the left in the fir trees came a howl and two yips; then answering yips came from the other side of the road.

"Coyotes."

Stephen shivered. "Do they come close?"

"Sure," Louie said with an offhand shrug. "But they're afraid of us so they're not dangerous."

The coyotes were joined by another and another until there was a chorus as untamed and distant as stars, yet eerily close.

"They do that when they make a kill," Louie said. "It's a signal for the others to join in."

"What do they kill?"

"Rabbits and mice, mostly. But sometimes they bring down a deer if it's wounded or sick."

The truck continued until finally Louie pointed.

"Look," he said. "There it is."

Ahead on the crest of a hill loomed a large house surrounded by trees. Below it was a circle of silver light; beyond the circle, a triangle of dark mountain.

"The lake," Louie said.

But Stephen thought of a silver cup lying at the foot of a huge pyramid, an offering at a giant's tomb. Everything in the mountains seemed made for giants.

The truck turned off the road onto another, then rattled through a field — there was no driveway — and stopped. Stephen picked up his knapsack and followed Louie through an unlocked door into a large log house. Uncle Adam came behind with the suitcases.

"I'll show you around," Louie said, switching on the lights and swaggering through the rooms, proud of the house he'd helped his parents build.

Three years ago, when they had put up the house, Louie hadn't been able to do much more than fetch tools and sweep up shavings, but since then he'd learned to peel logs and chisel corners for the log garage his father was building, so he could rightly say that some of this was his doing. He took Stephen into the main room first and switched on the lights.

"This is it," he said and watched Stephen's face for admiration. It was a beautiful room. Stephen's mouth went into a big O as he stared at the high ceilings, the leather chairs, the cedar tables, the log walls hung with weavings. High on the wall over the fireplace was a large wooden mask. His parents must have known about this mask: that was why they had sent the book. The mask was a large reddish disc with a raised circle face on it and orange rays came out from the face. It looked like an Indian mask Stephen had once seen in the museum.

"It's a sun mask," Louie said. "Old Angus carved it. He calls it the giver-of-life mask. He carved a moon mask too, but Mad took it with her on the bus."

"Who's Old Angus?" Stephen said.

"He's a mask carver who lives on the other side of the lake."

Stephen couldn't take his eyes off the mask: he wanted to try it on. He thought that if he could see through those eyes, breathe through that nose, speak through that mouth the world would look different — *he* would be different. Stephen had always been interested in masks. At home in his bedroom closet he still kept a dress-up box stocked with fake hair, false noses and plastic ears. There were discarded Hallowe'en masks: a red devil, a pirate, a gorilla. Sometimes he propped a mirror on top of his bureau and painted on a moustache and beard or used his sister's lipstick to draw a jagged red scar across his cheek. He didn't know why he did this. It had something to do with liking to pretend he was someone else, the freedom he felt escaping from himself.

Louie urged him away from the mask.

''C'mon, I'll show you the studio.''

He led the way into a large rectangular room built as a separate wing onto the back of the house. The room was filled with carved wooden boxes, book-ends, mugs, plates, ladles, lamps with handmade lampshades, woven hangings and cloths, runners, napkins, placemats—all carefully arranged on shelves and tables. At the far end of the room was a loom.

''This is where my mother works,'' Louie explained. ''People like to see her working when they come to buy. My father works in the basement.''

They went back into the main building and prowled around the bedrooms. There were two on the main floor: one was Mad's and the other belonged to Louie's parents. Louie slept upstairs in a large loft. Uncle Adam had already carried up the suitcases and set them on the floor.

Stephen looked around the loft. There were three windows, one looking out at the silver lake and the mountain, the others into trees. Beneath one of these windows was a shelf for games — Monopoly and Risk — for toy guns and soldiers, for spacecraft models. There was one book, *Mysteries of Outer Space*. Stephen guessed Louie didn't like to read much.

There were two sets of bunk beds in the room.

"You could sleep an army up here," Stephen said.

"You could," Louie said, "but there's never anyone but me." He sounded wistful.

He sat on the bunk.

Stephen took the book out of the knapsack to give to his aunt and uncle. Then on impulse he reached in, took out his new jack-knife and gave it to Louie.

Louie opened the knife and rubbed the shiny blade with his forefinger, pleased with the feel of cold metal against his skin. He closed the blade and put it in his pocket. Then he stood up and went downstairs.

In the large kitchen Aunt Lise was making hot chocolate and cinnamon toast. The room was cosy, heated by an old-fashioned wood-burning stove. There was a long plank table with benches instead of chairs. Stephen gave the book to his uncle, since he was the carver.

"Well thanks," his uncle said. He sat down at the table and opened the book. "I wonder what Angus would think of this," he mused.

Aunt Lise turned from the wood stove with another mug of chocolate, her face shining and pink from the heat.

"Not much, probably," she said. "You know he's an instinctive carver. Primitive."

"Not much given to words, written or spoken," Uncle Adam agreed and slowly turned the pages.

"Is that why he lives in the woods?" Stephen asked. "Because he's primitive?"

"Guess so," Uncle Adam said, then quickly amended. "It's not that *he's* primitive, but his masks are."

"Do you know him?" Stephen said.

"Not very well. He keeps to himself. We've seen him only a couple of times when we've gone over to buy masks." Uncle Adam turned another page. "I think Mrs Riley knows him as well as anybody around here. The Rileys have lived here for years. They pioneered this valley."

Aunt Lise handed Stephen a slice of toast.

While he ate, Stephen wandered from room to room, sprinkling sugar and cinnamon as he went. He could see this was the sort of home where you could do this. He liked it here: the log walls, hung with weavings and the mask, were so different from the walls at home. Hung with mirrors and curtains, his house seemed to be on another planet.

After they had eaten more toast, Aunt Lise shunted them off to bed.

When they were in their bunks, their stomachs warm and full, Stephen said, "Do you think we could cross the lake tomorrow and see Old Angus? I'd sure like to see how he carves his masks."

"Maybe," Louie yawned. He wasn't all that eager to see Angus again. He was used to watching his father work. He didn't particularly want to watch another carver. He hoped that he and Stephen would like doing the same things. A whole month together would be a drag if they didn't. He had already made their summer plans: swimming, scouting the lake bottom for salvage, working in his tree-lab, camping, hiking up to the cave. But he guessed they could manage a visit to Angus. "We'll see him sometime," he said sleepily. He had worked hard all day getting the place ready for his cousin's visit. He was tired. He fell asleep.

Stephen lay on his bunk thinking about the sun mask. If he tried it on, would everything look brighter, warmer? Louie had said Mad had taken a moon mask to his house in the city. If she put it on, would it make everything smooth and silver the way the moonlight was doing now, carving the bunk posts into marble columns, transforming the empty bunk opposite into a silver meadow? Again he wondered what it would be like to wear the sun mask. He imagined himself wearing it.

He was high in the sky. Below him everything pulsed with energy and life. Trees suddenly sprang up, lifting fragrant green branches towards him. A lake appeared, swelling with large, sleek fish. A mountain opened up, and out spilled people wearing masks. He saw someone dressed like a large bird gather the people together. Though there were only a few clouds drifting around him, Stephen heard the drum roll of thunder. The people began to dance to the drumming. Every now and then someone would look up and wave a rattle at him. Stephen smiled. Each time he smiled, the masked people danced faster and more wildly, until he saw sweat glistening on their bodies. He smiled on. Eventually the people danced back into the mountain, and Stephen saw that, except for himself, the sky was empty. He went to sleep.

Two

Stephen and Louie slept late. At noon they awoke to find the loft suffused in amber light. Sunlight shone through the window and fell on the log walls and pine floor. The air was warm. A yellow jacket buzzed against the screen. Outside the circle of fir trees a light breeze sighed. Beyond the trees the lake shimmered, as if thousands of fish were flicking their golden tails.

Louie looked across the room.

''Want to go swimming?'' he said.

Stephen stretched lazily.

''Sure.''

They slithered out of bed and undressed, taking in the strangeness of each other's bodies. Stephen was tall and lanky; his fair skin was freckled, and fuzzed with reddish-blond hair. Louie was shorter, sturdier and darkly tanned.

Louie put on his bathing suit and stepped into his jeans. Both knees were out. His mother was a good weaver but a terrible sewer. He took off the jeans, went downstairs and came back with scissors, which he used to sever the legs, converting the jeans into cutoffs. He slipped these on over his bathing suit, unconcerned that one leg of the cutoffs was longer than the other. Then he put on a faded T-shirt with a hole under one arm.

Stephen tore the price tag off his yellow bathing suit and put it on. Over it he slipped a pair of neatly cuffed shorts. He pulled on a bright yellow shirt with Stampede City on its front. His clothes smelled new; he had been saving them for this trip.

Barefoot, both boys padded downstairs to the kitchen. At the back of the woodstove, oatmeal warmed in a pan of hot water Aunt Lise had put there before going into her studio. Louie got down bowls and spooned out sticky porridge. He put a tin of brown sugar on the table and a carton of milk, tossed down two spoons. Louie moved about the kitchen with a careless confidence. This impressed Stephen, who was not encouraged to cook in the kitchen at home because he might mess it up. Louie stoked the fire, added a log from the box beside the stove, straddled one of the benches at the table and sat down to eat. When their oatmeal was gone, Louie removed the stove lid, put a wire grate over the opening and began to make toast, turning it with a fork. They ate the toast with a tart red jelly Stephen had never tasted before.

"Chokecherry," Louie offered. "Mrs Riley made it. We sell it in our shop. Marmalade too."

Some of the jelly dribbled onto Stephen's new shirt. He sponged it off with the dishrag. Louie put the dishes in the sink and sloshed water over them. Then he went into the bathroom for towels, and the boys went outside. On the back doorstep they stopped and sniffed the air like spring cubs. It was soft and clear and light. They ambled down the side of the house past a screen door that opened from the basement workshop. Stephen saw his uncle's hand lift in greeting, but Louie didn't even glance that way. His father had promised him a free day to show Stephen around. He didn't want to spend any of it inside.

They stepped outside the circle of trees, and Stephen saw the golden lake. Beyond it towered the pyramidal mountain. The mountain was heavily treed except on its shoulders, which were grey rock with snow on them. Low on the mountain, where the trees were thickest, was a curious blurred spot that was a shade darker than the forest surrounding it. The spot was indistinct as if it were no more than the shadow of a passing cloud.

Stephen pointed. "What's that up there?"

"It's a cave," Louie said. "When you're out on the lake you can see it better. Sometimes you can't see it at all. It depends on how the light hits it."

"Have you been up there?"

"Not yet," Louie said. "It's one of the things I was planning to do when you got here. It's farther away than it looks. C'mon, I'll show you my tree-lab." He ran down the slope, unmindful of the prickly grass underfoot. Stephen, whose feet were tender, took longer.

The tree-lab was built between four fir trees at the water's edge. Louie had built it so that it overlooked the dock. Louie threw the towels onto the dock and climbed a ladder to the tree-lab. Stephen followed and got a splinter in his heel. Next time he'd wear his Nikes.

The tree-lab was a room with a roof on top. It was a first-class job, Louie said, because his father had let him use good siding instead of leftover wood. The walls were straight and evenly matched. The two sides had large windows for light, the back wall was solid and the front wall had a door with a padlock on it.

Louie stood on the top rung and unlocked the door. They crawled into the room. The inside of the tree-lab was neat and orderly. On the back wall were shelves, and on them rows of jam and pickle jars that had been washed clean and had their labels soaked off. The jars held grasshoppers, moths, water spiders in swamp water, cocoons, caterpillars, a snake and a frog. On one of the shelves were four monarch butterflies pressed under glass. Stephen didn't like the butterflies.

Louie saw him looking at them. ''I kill them with chloroform,'' he said. ''It's quick. Then I press them for my mother, who uses them to decorate lampshades.''

Stephen didn't like the thought of killing helpless butterflies, even for lampshades.

Stephen heard a car door slam. He looked out the window into the trees.

''Who's that?''

''Campers, probably. Mrs Riley has a campground next door,'' Louie said. ''C'mon, I'll show you my salvage bin.'' He locked the tree-lab door and they backed down the ladder. Louie had worn a path through the bushes to the dock. They followed it to a wooden box Louie had built beside the bulrushes. Inside it was a rubber tire crusted with dried sediment from the lake bottom, a coil of rusty barbed wire, a man's boot, a plastic gallon jug, jagged cans, pop tins and broken beer bottles.

''This is what I've taken from the lake bottom so far,'' he said. ''Just in this cove, and I'm not done yet. There's a big barrel I still have to get out.''

''Who put all this stuff into the lake?''

''Who knows?'' Louie shrugged. ''Some people will dump their garbage anywhere.''

Guiltily Stephen remembered last year's school

campout, when he'd hidden his lunch bag and pop tin behind a rock at the end of the trail so he wouldn't have to hike back out with them.

"What are you going to do with it all?"

Louie shrugged. "Don't know yet. Bury it, maybe," he said, though he knew that, even buried, the glass wouldn't decompose. You could shoot bottles out in space and still they'd be garbage orbiting the earth with all the cast-off hardware. There were some things you couldn't get rid of no matter how hard you tried.

They passed the firepit used for family cookouts and stepped onto the dock.

Stephen looked at the lake. Here in the cove the water was the colour of lime Jell-O, cool and inviting, so different from city pools chlorinated the colour of Windex. There was a raft half-way out in the cove.

"Is that yours?" he said.

"Yup. We take the boat out to it," Louie said. "Water's deeper there. Better for diving."

They strolled to the end of the dock.

"Where are our towels?" Louie said.

They weren't where he had thrown them.

There was a snigger from inside the bulrushes.

Stephen looked in the boat, a red dory with *The Explorer* painted on its side in black letters. He looked in the water.

"They're gone," he said.

There was a second snigger.

Another and another.

Louie glared at the bulrushes.

"All right, Willard. We want our towels."

"We want our towels," mimicked the voice.

Stephen felt his heart, which had been high with the anticipation of a perfect day, take an ominous downward turn. Bullies. There were bullies here. This was one of the things he was escaping from at home. He hadn't expected to meet bullies. He thought there must be some places where there weren't any, and from the enthusiastic letters his aunt had written to his mother describing the mountain valley and the lake, he had thought this must be such a place. He looked at his cousin to see how he was taking it. Louie had his arms folded, his feet apart. He looked cross, impatient, annoyed at the inconvenience.

"You heard what I said," he ordered them. "Hand over our towels."

"Come and get them," a voice singsonged.

Louie recognized Sludge's voice. He was in there with Willard. He decided to call their bluff.

"Ah, we don't need towels. The sun'll dry us. C'mon, Steve. Give me a hand with this boat."

It belonged to Mad, but Louie was allowed to use it if he was careful.

As he bent over to help lift the dory into the water, Stephen felt a thud against the back of his new yellow shirt. When he straightened up, another handful of wet muck and slime landed on Stampede City.

"That's enough, you jerks," Louie said.

A blob of slime splattered his old blue shirt.

He set the oars in their locks.

"Let's go, Steve," he said.

The bulrushes parted and two boys stood up. Armed with bulrushes, they stepped onto the dock, their runners caked with mud and slime. One of the boys had curly gold hair, full pink cheeks and a round belly. Even with the smirk on his face he looked like a choirboy. This was Sludge.

Willard, the boy beside him, was tall and whip thin. His face was brown and sullen, the hair on his neck tufted up like a grouse tail.

Willard jerked a thumb at Stephen.

"Who's this geek?" he said.

"He's my cousin. He's staying with me for a month," Louie said.

"What a patsy," Willard sneered. "Stampede City. Big deal." He lifted the bulrush and switched it sideways across Stephen's arm. "How do you like that, city boy?"

Stephen put a hand on his arm where he'd been hit. Beneath it the skin was red and hot, rising to a welt. He kept his eyes down. He had blue eyes that watered easily. He didn't want them to think he was crying.

"Lay off him, you guys," Louie said. "He never did a thing to you."

"Lay off him, you guys, he never did a thing to you," repeated Willard.

He brought the bulrush switch across Louie's leg.

Louie reached out and pushed Willard backwards into the bulrushes. Sludge gave Louie a shove, but Louie kept his feet. He got an armlock on Sludge's neck and wrestled him into the water, where Sludge spluttered and splashed like a convulsive hippo.

"I can't swim!" he yelled. "I can't swim!"

"So I noticed," Louie said.

And was given a push by Willard. But Louie had looked behind him in time and managed to get a hold on Willard's waist. They fell into the water together. Willard couldn't swim either. He stood up, churning up the silty bottom with his feet. The water came up to his chest. He waded to the dock while Louie swam to deeper water.

Stephen got into the dory. He was a good swimmer, but he thought that if he was in the boat it would be harder for the bullies to throw him into the lake, where they might hold his head under or do something mean like that. Willard didn't even look at him. He cupped his hands over his mouth and yelled out over the water at Louie, "You wait, we'll get you for this!"

But Louie didn't hear him.

Stephen watched as Willard and Sludge, who had hauled himself spluttering and gasping out of the water, walked into the bushes, leaving a trail of wet footprints on the dock.

When they had disappeared into the trees separating the Barrows' land from the campground, Stephen crept out of the dory and looked in the bulrushes for their towels. He took them to the side of the dock where the water hadn't been stirred up and washed off the slime. He wrung them out and spread them across the seats in the dory to dry. Then he got in and pushed off.

Louie was swimming a large circle around the cove, ignoring him. Stephen took his time rowing out to the raft. He rowed to the opposite side of the cove where the water was shallowest, a clear lemon yellow. Stephen peered over the side of the dory. He saw that Louie's salvage operations had shaken up the lake bottom, and like the snow in a glass paperweight, the silt had resettled into mysterious patterns. He saw the outline of a footprint. The edges of the footprint were blurred, indistinct. Perhaps it was only a scuffmark. He rowed on. The water went from yellow to lime green to dark blue. The raft was anchored where green and blue met.

Louie had come back and was sitting on the raft edge, feet in the water, his clothes in a wet heap beside him. Stephen climbed out of *The Explorer* and tied it to a nail on the raft beside a sign that said PRIVATE. Still Louie said nothing. But as soon as Stephen had slipped out of his clothes, Louie pushed him into the water.

"Hey!" Stephen yelled. He held his breath and went under. He bobbed up laughing. He grabbed Louie's foot and pulled him in. They trod water and looked at each other. Stephen shoved Louie's head underwater.

Louie surfaced and shook his head, sleek and dark as a seal's.

"Why didn't you do that to Willard?" he said.

"Willard?"

"Willard Soper, the guy who hit you. The other one's Sludge Riley."

"I don't know," Stephen said.

"You should have pushed him into the water," Louie insisted. "You should have shown him. It was what he needed."

"Maybe it's because I just got here," Stephen said. "Maybe it's because I'm not used to this place yet."

"Maybe," Louie said. He sounded doubtful. He smacked his hand against the water, spraying Stephen's eyes.

"Race you to the cove mouth," he said.

Stephen won the race, which made everything all right again.

They dived underwater and Louie showed him the rusty barrel.

Afterwards they lay on the raft on their towels, which smelled swampy but at least were dry. Shivering, they burrowed into the towels like desert creatures into sand while the sun gilded their bodies in molten light. Around them the water gleamed Nile green and ebony, as smooth as liquid glass. Mating dragonflies swooped overhead, their long tails curled into strings of Egyptian beads. The boys closed their eyes, their features slipping into golden repose as inscrutable as Pharoahs' masks. For a long time they lay in sunlight. And then from across the water at Riley's there came the blast of a transistor radio.

"Sludge and Willard aren't your friends, are they?" Stephen said.

Louie's head jerked up.

"You kidding? More like enemies. I haven't got any friends. At least," he added quickly, "when I'm not in school I haven't. Out here you have school friends and home friends. See?" Before Stephen could answer, he said, "C'mon, if we stay here much longer we'll melt."

They jumped off the raft, squealing, their hot bodies slapping the cool water. Stephen floated on his back and looked at the pyramidal mountain, at the cave drawing him in like one eye inside another.

"Let's eat!" Louie shouted into his ear.

Later, after they had gone back to the house to eat jam sandwiches and drink a quart of Kool-Aid, they returned to the water. This time Louie brought his snorkel equipment, flippers and a coil of rope. They took turns, one of them rowing, the other negotiating the rope around the rusty barrel. The barrel was deeply embedded in silt, which made it difficult to lasso. They used sticks to pry it loose. This stirred up the water so they had to wait for the sediment to settle before they could try again. Eventually they got the barrel out of the lake and into the salvage bin.

For supper they cooked hot dogs in the firepit. Aunt Lise brought bowls of tossed salad, which they washed down with mugs of milk. Afterwards Uncle Adam rowed all of them across the glassy lake towards the opposite shore, where there was a beaver dam. They waited in the darkening light for the beaver to appear, but he never did. The sun had dipped behind the mountains; the water's edge was deep in shadow. This gave the lake a sunken, hidden look. On their way back, Stephen looked up at the cave, but the black eye had merged with the shadows. Near the dock they saw a pair of loons glide out of the bulrushes and across the polished surface of the lake. ''They look like dancers at a masquerade ball,'' Aunt Lise said.

One of the loons lifted its head and called mysteriously into the darkening night.

Three

*T*hat night Stephen's sunburn kept him awake. The skin on his back was bright red. The welt on his arm smarted. If he lay on his back, his burn hurt. If he lay on his stomach, his arm hurt. It was too hot for sheets, so he lay there feeling alternately hot and shivery. Moonlight streamed through the window, making light patches and dark corners in the room. One of the light patches was Louie's sleeping face. Tanned brown in sunlight, it was now cast in silver.

What made it worse was that every time Stephen closed his eyes he saw Willard's sneering face and hostile eyes. Stephen pushed the face away, but Willard kept coming back. The harder Stephen pushed, the bigger the face loomed, the sneer widening, the eyes mocking.

Stephen reached out and stuck his fingertips into those mocking eyes. The eyeballs popped back as if they were on springs, and Stephen's fingertips touched something soft and jellylike inside Willard's head. Then he yanked Willard's body across the dock. He had seen a fisherman do this once on TV, poke his hands right into the eyes of a big fish, hooking his fingers into the sockets, dragging the fish across the wharf. Stephen shuddered with revulsion at this picture. You should have shown him, *he heard Louie say.* It was what he needed. *The voice was hollow, as if it were coming from inside a mask. Stephen shifted to his side, willing the cool moonlight to pour over him, to mould him into a metallic tube, long and smooth as a missile. Something mindless that didn't think such scary thoughts. But then a picture of himself astride Sludge sprang into his head. He was wearing his Stampede City shirt and a pair of cowboy boots with spurs on them. He was digging the spurs into Sludge's fat hide and shouting, "Ride, Hippo, ride!" and Sludge was bucking up and down in the shallows of the lake, crashing into the bulrushes, wallowing in the mud.*

Stephen blinked and shook his head trying to get rid of these nightmare pictures, but it was no use. Every time he closed his eyes they came back again, flashing on his mind screen in livid colour.

It was the same every time he was bullied.

Whenever Terry Mulcaster, the bully next door at home, helped himself to Stephen's lunch, his compass set or his gym shirt, Stephen seemed

powerless to stop him. Terry was always break-
ing into Stephen's locker. Once, after Stephen
reported him to the principal, Terry jumped him
as he was riding home on his bike. He gave him
a black eye and six broken wheel spokes. Stephen
didn't fight back. It was the same every time he
was bullied. When someone belted him, he
couldn't hit back. He stood there and took it. He
couldn't seem to move his body into action. It
wasn't that he hadn't tried. Over and over he'd
gone outside to ride his bike, play ball, play street
hockey, resolving to fight back if someone bullied him, but he never did. They poked and
taunted him and still he could do nothing. Afterwards he had these violent revenges. They reeled
across his mind like horror movies, terrifying him
with his own cruelty. The only way of avoiding
these nightmares was to avoid bullies, to take the
long way home, to stay inside, to amuse himself
with TV and books, which was how he increas-
ingly spent his time. He knew this was why his
mother had been urging him to spend a month
with his cousin in the mountains. She didn't say
this. What she said with her usual briskness was,
all that fresh air and sunshine will do you good. If she
could only see what sunshine had done to him
now, made him red as a boiled lobster.

Stephen kept his eyes open to keep the nightmares away. He noticed that the empty bunk
above Louie was in moonlight; both he and Louie
occupied lower bunks. The moonlight angled

through the window so that a shaft fell on his cousin's face, but most of it fell on the bunk above. Stephen picked up his pillow and moved across to the top bunk. There, curled up on his good arm, he turned his face towards the window and willed the moonlight to slide a silver sleep mask over his face.

When Stephen awoke, Louie was already downstairs in the kitchen eating breakfast with his father. Stephen dressed quickly and joined them. He felt hot and heavy headed. A blast of warm air from the wood stove hit him as he entered the kitchen. It made him feel woozy.

"Looks like you overdid the sun," Uncle Adam said. "Louie, fetch the cocoa butter."

Louie got the jar of cream from the bathroom, and Uncle Adam oiled Stephen's shoulders and arms in soothing strokes. Stephen shivered.

"You'd better stay inside today," Uncle Adam advised.

"Aw Dad," Louie said. "We've got exploring to do."

"You heard me. Any more sun and your cousin will be sick in bed. You boys can help me downstairs. Your mother's got her hands full with the craft fair that's coming up, so first you'd better clean up the kitchen."

After breakfast the boys washed the dishes and wiped the crumbs off the table. Then they went downstairs to the workroom using a set of stairs beside the back door. The basement was cool and smelled of wood shavings. The workroom was the front half of the basement. It had a row of long windows opening into the circle of trees; beneath that was a long bench with stools in front of it and a rack for chisels, knives and mallets. A vise was mounted on the end of the bench and beside it a lathe. Strips of sandpaper and shavings littered the floor. Wood was stacked against one wall: irregular blocks of cedar, aspen, pine. Uncle Adam worked on a stool in front of the side door. He was sanding a long spoon. The spoon had a snake coiled around its bowl. For a while the boys stood silently and watched him carve. Uncle Adam had sure hands that moved quickly, scoring the handle to make it look like scales, then deepening these lines into furrows. Louie got bored first.

"C'mon, let's get the work over with," he said. "You sweep and I'll put things away." He handed Stephen the broom. Then he began straightening up the bench.

When they were done, Uncle Adam said, "I'd like you to oil a pair of lamp bases for me." He put down the spoon and the knife, rummaged around until he found a tin of oil and rags. The lamp bases had miniature scenes carved in them. One was a boy on a dock fishing, the other a girl in a boat rowing. The scenes were carved deep into the wood, and the depth gave them a three-dimensional effect. Every detail had been carved, even the clouds in the sky. Uncle Adam handed Stephen the rowing girl and Louie the fishing boy.

"Make sure you get into all the grooves," he said. "And don't glob on too much oil. Use a bit at a time and rub it in until the wood shines."

They spent the rest of the morning sitting in the green silence, rubbing and polishing. Stephen felt good being in the workshop. The coolness eased his sunburn, and it was satisfying to see how the oil brought out the details.

Outside they heard a door open, voices.

"Customers," Uncle Adam said. "Maybe you should go up and see if you can help your mother."

Upstairs they found Aunt Lise stirring milk into three mugs of tea. She gave one to a fat woman who was sitting at the plank table. The other she gave to Louie.

"Take that downstairs to your father," she said. Then she turned to the fat woman. "Ardelle, this is our nephew, Stephen. He's visiting us from the city. Stephen, this is Mrs Riley."

The fat woman beamed. "Glad to meet you, Stephen," she said. She had a plump, good-natured face, a pompadour of witchily black hair and hoop earrings.

He wondered what relation this woman was to Sludge.

"Mrs Riley has been kind enough to bring me some flowers for my lampshades," Aunt Lise said.

Stephen noticed a clear plastic folder on the table containing pressed flowers.

"You'll have to meet my grandson, Edward," Mrs Riley said in a rich, throaty voice. She smiled encouragingly.

"Does Edward have a twin?" Stephen asked.

Mrs Riley laughed. Her hoop earrings swung to and fro.

"Why no. A good thing, too. Edward is more than I can handle."

Aunt Lise looked perplexed. "What made you think he had a twin?" she said.

Stephen laughed. "Just wondering."

Louie had come back upstairs and was nudging Stephen's elbow. Louie felt uncomfortable around Mrs Riley. He always felt on the verge of blurting out how two-faced Sludge was.

"Let's play Risk," he said.

They went up to the loft.

Stephen had never played Risk.

"I'll show you," Louie said. He took the game off the shelf and spread it on the floor.

"The idea is to conquer the world," he said. He set out the cards, the dice and the army pieces.

Stephen picked up the instruction booklet and read: "Players take turns initiating battles. Each battle can have three parts. One, deploying enemies; two, attacking the opposition; three, fortifying the territories held." Louie gave Stephen the dice. "Roll to see who goes first."

They began to play, keeping the door ajar so

they could hear the conversation going on below.

Most of it was about Mrs Riley's campers, her bird-watching — she kept a record of each new bird that came to the lake — and the craft fair that was being held in the village the day after tomorrow. Mrs Riley was planning to sell flower arrangements and her jams and jellies at the fair.

"Though, heaven knows, the little money I earn from the sale will come in one door and go out the other," Mrs Riley sighed. "Every time I turn around, Edward is asking me for money to buy gas for his motorbike. But maybe it's worth it. At least the motorbike keeps him out of trouble."

"You go first," Louie said.

"Of course he's *supposed* to be earning money for gas by doing chores around the campground, but you know how kids are about doing chores." There was another heavy sigh. "It's hard raising a boy at my age."

"It must be," Aunt Lise sympathized. Then she went on about her mother, Marie Delphine, who had raised her sister Louise and herself single-handedly.

Louie conquered Egypt and the Middle East, then fortified them with fourteen armies. Stephen conquered Venezuela and Peru. They concentrated on the game until they heard Mrs Riley say, "I don't know what got into him out there in the middle of the lake with a mask on. He nearly frightened me out of my wits.''

"She's talking about Angus," Louie whispered.

Stephen put down the dice and listened.

''I know his masks are beautiful, works of art and all that,'' Mrs Riley said. ''But I don't think wearing them just anywhere he pleases is the thing to do. Especially out on the lake. What if I'd moved too fast and tipped the boat? I would have drowned.''

"When was this?'' Aunt Lise wanted to know.

''Last night. I was across the lake in the reeds bird-watching, trying to get a peek at the bittern that's nesting there. I've been wanting to see one for years. They're such shy birds, you know. I waited and waited until it got too dark to see properly, but I could hear it cry. Pump-er-link, pump-er-link.'' Mrs Riley sounded as if she had swallowed a frog.

Stephen and Louie snorted with laughter but capped it before the old woman could hear.

''That's funny,'' Aunt Lise said. ''We were out on the lake at dusk and I didn't see you.''

''I was probably hidden by the reeds. Anyway, just as it was getting quite dark,'' Mrs Riley said, ''who would come sliding out of the reeds but Angus, wearing one of his scary masks. He moved that quiet I didn't see him until his canoe was smack behind me. I turned and there was this face, half red and half black, with a twisted mouth, staring at me. 'My goodness,' I said, '*who* or *what* are you?' And do you know what he said?''

''What?''

Mrs Riley's voice went very deep. '' 'I am the Great World Being.' Imagine! So I said, 'What in the world is *that*?' '' Her voice deepened again. '' 'I am the morning and the evening. I scatter my ashes. I bring good to the world.' What is a person supposed to make of that gobbledygook? I said, 'You'll do no good if you scare me to death. Then you'll have a dead body on your hands.' That shook him. Too close for comfort, I guess. Not that I intended to dig up the past.''

''What do you mean, 'dig up the past'?''

''Oh my, I shouldn't have said that,'' Mrs Riley dithered. Her voice dropped out of hearing. The boys strained to hear. Mrs Riley's voice was like a mountain range: all peaks and valleys. She stayed in the valley only for a moment, then soared upward. ''Anyway, I told him, 'There are *other* people using this lake, and you might scare them too.' ''

''I should think so,'' Aunt Lise agreed.

''He didn't seem to take any notice of what I said. He asked me if I'd seen the beaver lately and I said no. Then he asked me if Mel Soper had trapped it, and I told him not to my knowledge he hadn't. Angus always had a soft spot for beavers. When my husband Bert was alive he trapped a big one that was piling brush in front of the culvert and flooding our well. Angus pried the trap loose and carried the beaver fifteen miles up the valley to another lake. 'Hated to see anything cooped up,' he said. I suppose that comes from once being cooped up himself.'' Mrs Riley paused to gulp in air, then went on, ''I don't want Angus scaring my campers. I mean, if they saw him going through all that rigmarole out on the lake, well, they wouldn't be likely to want to come back here again, now would they? I hope he stays put in the woods the next time he decides to put on one of his masks.'' Mrs Riley sighed. ''He's a strange one, all right.''

''How long have you known Angus?'' Aunt Lise said.

''My goodness, it seems forever. As far back as I can remember he's been over there on the other side of the lake. He was there when Bert's father homesteaded this valley. Though Bert did say Angus had done a lot of other things in his life — worked his way around the world on freighters, was up north in the bush, was even in a travelling circus. Seems he has itchy feet. Every so often he takes off someplace. Disappears. Where, I couldn't say. But he always comes back.''

''But where did he come from in the first place?'' Aunt Lise persisted.

''I wouldn't know. I wasn't born in these parts but down the valley a ways. I think of Angus the way I do the mountain. He's part of the wilderness. I remember Bert saying there was a tribe of Indians over there once a long time ago. Maybe he's what's left of them.''

"I thought maybe Angus came from the coast,'' Aunt Lise put in. "That's where the best wooden-mask carvers are. I thought maybe he had learned how to carve there.''

"I should think a person could learn to carve masks anywhere there are trees,'' Mrs Riley said tartly.

Stephen heard Mrs Riley shove back the bench she was sitting on. It scraped loudly against the floor.

"Well, I've got to be going,'' she said. "I want to make a few more flower arrangements for the fair.''

After she had left, Stephen and Louie went back to Risk. Louie conquered all of Africa and Madagascar; Stephen, Central and South America. Between them they amassed 154 armies. They kept on until the world had been conquered. Only then did they leave the game and go downstairs. On the way down, Stephen looked at the sun mask. The eyes seemed to see through him, through the thick walls of the house. He wondered if Angus had tried on this mask before selling it to the Barrows.

Aunt Lise was in the kitchen making tuna sandwiches.

"I have to go into the village for groceries,''

she said. "I want you boys to tend the shop for me while I'm gone."

Louie groaned.

"You may as well," she said. "I don't want Stephen in that hot sun until his sunburn eases. He can probably go out tomorrow."

When she'd rattled away in the pickup, Louie took his stack of comics, and they went outside and sat on the steps in the shade to read and eat their sandwiches.

After a while a black Mercedes rolled over the scruffy tracks towards them and parked. A middle-aged man and woman got out and strolled into the shop.

Louie glanced at their black and gold licence plate and muttered, "Yellow jackets."

Stephen thought he meant hornets. He ducked nervously.

"The licence plates," Louie said. "That's what we call them out there."

Out there. These people were from Calgary. Stephen followed Louie inside and sat on the bench in front of the loom.

After a brief inspection the man went back outside. His wife oh'd and ah'd over the carvings and weavings. Stephen felt strangely embarrassed by the woman. He didn't want to be reminded that she came from the same place he did. Already he thought of her as an intruder. But the woman had no such claim on Louie. He was used to tourists coming and going. The city where he had once lived no longer took up a large part of him. Besides, the woman was buying a set of place-mats with matching napkins and a wall hanging. His mother would be pleased.

"You have such lovely things," the woman gushed. "Does this place belong to your parents, dear?"

Louie told her. He made the business sound like a family project.

"My, my." The woman added a large wooden salad bowl and four smaller bowls to her purchases.

Louie wrapped the items in newspaper and packed them neatly inside a brown grocery bag. The woman carried the bag outside to her husband, who was waiting in the car.

No sooner had they driven away than Aunt Lise rumbled across the field, the back of the truck filled with groceries. The boys helped her carry the bags inside and unpack them. Stephen folded the bags flat for use in the shop, and Louie put things away. Aunt Lise unpacked the last bag herself.

"I bought some fresh strawberries, whipping cream and a bag of ice," she said. "Louie, fetch the bucket. We're making strawberry ice cream for a treat, or rather *you* are. I'm making a sponge cake."

That night they celebrated Louie's big sale. Aunt Lise made real lemonade, which they drank with hamburgers she had cooked. After supper they sat on the front porch in the cool evening air eating strawberry ice cream and soft chunks of sponge cake, watching the blue mantle of dusk gradually enfold the mountain, turning its peak from rose gold to mauve blue and finally to grey black. The cave changed, too. It looked like a closing eye, like a window over which a shade was being lowered. As the shade came down, Stephen felt his eyelids droop. Soon he was following Louie upstairs to bed.

Four

T he next morning the sun rose, a gleaming ball of fire, its rays reaching deep into the loft.

Louie was first to waken. He was already in his bathing suit when his mother called up.

"Tell Stephen not to take off his shirt today even when he's swimming and to wear a hat." Then she went into her studio and shut the door. Louie's father was already in his workshop.

Downstairs in the hall closet they found a peaked cap; it was from Uncle Adam's golf-playing days. Stephen put on the cap. After they bolted down their oatmeal and toast, they went outside into the summer sunlight. Stephen carried the towels, and Louie the flippers and mask.

The Barrows' log house was on top of a hill, a long bare slope that ended in trees at the water's

edge. A ditch ran parallel to the slope. It was an
irrigation ditch built by Sludge Riley's grand-
father, who had once tried to grow apple trees in
the rocky mountain soil. The ditch had long since
fallen into disuse. It was now filled with boul-
ders and stones. It was in this ditch that Sludge
and Willard were hiding. They waited until Louie
and Stephen were well down the slope, out of
their parents' hearing yet some distance from the
water's safety, before they came rumbling out of
the ditch on their motorbikes. Disguised in gog-
gles and bubble helmets, they could have been
Hell's Angels roaring down pavement, Spitfire
pilots screaming an attack, Black Knights zero-
ing through space.

"Stick together," Louie muttered, but it was
too late.

Stephen was already rooted to the spot; Louie
had moved on. Willard zoomed between them
on his motorbike, like a cowboy cutting out a
calf for branding. He rode in tight circles around
Stephen, who stood mute, clutching the towels.
Dust puffed out from beneath Willard's tires, coat-
ing Stephen's clean Nikes. There was a sneer on
Willard's face as he drew the circle smaller and
smaller, his motorbike coming so close that his
shoulder brushed Stephen's sore arm.

Stephen saw Louie run in sudden bursts down
the hill, making it difficult for Sludge to draw a
noose around him. Stephen tried to do the same,
but Willard kept intercepting him. His front wheel

ran across Stephen's toe. Stephen stopped, his cheeks burning with rage and humiliation.

Louie had reached the bottom of the slope and was heading towards thick bushes. When he got close enough, he held a long branch across Sludge's path so that when the motorbike circled around again, the branch snapped up and hit Sludge's chin. The motorbike veered off its path, and Louie made a dash for the tree-lab ladder. Sludge roared back up the hill to join Willard. The two of them gunned their machines in a tight knot around Stephen like two black crows circling a sparrow with a broken wing.

Louie scrambled up the ladder and opened the tree-lab door. He kept a pile of stones and a sling-shot up there for emergencies. He dropped down the ladder, fitted a rock in the sling and took aim. The rock landed squarely on Sludge's back. The fat boy howled. His machine wobbled off course and caught Willard as he came around the circle. Both machines stopped, their wheels spinning. Willard cursed loudly.

Stephen made a run for it. He didn't stop until he had reached the tree-lab ladder. He climbed up after Louie. Louie closed the door and they sat in the comforting green gloom. They heard the machines roar away. Stephen heard his heart banging against his ribs. After it subsided he said, ''Why do they hate us so much?''

''I don't know,'' Louie said. He didn't understand it, especially with Mrs Riley being so kind.

Ever since they'd moved here, Sludge and Willard had been giving him a hard time: throwing rocks at him, calling him names, taunting him. Behind Mrs Riley's back, of course. They acted as if he didn't belong here, as if this property weren't his family's, bought from Mrs Riley for a fair price. Obviously they didn't know the rules of Monopoly or Risk — that once you paid money for land, you owned it, and that once you owned it, you had the right to defend it.

"Wait a minute," Louie said. "I'll be right back."

Louie backed down the ladder and ran uphill. Stephen watched him slip through the circle of trees. Within minutes he was on his way back, running down the slope with a large board, a hammer, a red crayon and nails. When he reached the foot of the ladder he called up, "C'mon down. Lock the door after you and bring all our stuff."

By the time Stephen was back on the ground with the towels and the snorkel equipment, Louie had crayoned NO TRESPASSING on the board in large red letters. He propped the sign against a tree. Then he went to the salvage bin and pulled out the roll of rusty barbed wire.

"Help me string this along the property line," he said. They carried the wire into the bushes to where a row of stakes had been driven into the ground. Following this line they unrolled the wire and nailed it to the trees. There was enough wire to make a fence from the lake's edge through the trees to the tree-lab ladder. Louie hammered the NO TRESPASSING sign onto the largest tree.

"There!" he said, satisfied. "Now for a swim."

When they were in the boat Stephen pointed to the shallow side of the cove. "Row over there. I want to show you something."

Stephen didn't really expect the footprint to still be there. He thought that by this time it would be no more than a scuffmark roughly in the shape of a foot. He certainly never expected to see a second print embedded in the bottom, the heel and toes clearly outlined.

"See those?"

Louie looked over the edge of the dory into the clear yellow water and whistled.

"Do you suppose a Sasquatch could've made them?" Stephen said. "Or the Wendigo?" He had read all about wild giants that inhabited mountain wildernesses: Bigfoot, Dsonqua, the Yeti. All of them had big feet like this.

"Nah," Louie said. He didn't believe any of that stuff. "If they were footprints they'd be *going* somewhere."

"Unless it stood and then swam."

Louie thought this over. "Probably I made those marks when I was hauling all that junk out of the lake. I could have made them with a flipper."

"They aren't flipper shaped," Stephen said.

"They have toes. Besides, there's a new one that wasn't there the other day." He paused. "What's in this lake, anyway?"

"Trout. Minnows. That's all. But it's deep. It's fed by an underground stream. It's supposed to be bottomless."

In Stephen's mind *bottomless* conjured up lake monsters, Nessie and Ogopogo, sluggish creatures with huge mouths and prowling appetites.

They rowed to the raft and tied up the dory. Louie jumped into the water and struck out for deeper water. Because of his sunburn Stephen wanted to take his time getting into the water. He sat on the edge of the raft, leaned over and stared at his reflection in the glassy lake. Then he lay on his stomach, covered his sunburned arms with a towel and looked at himself again. The water magnified his face into an ugly monster's, one with salt-shaker-hole pores, bramble bush eyebrows and a mouth as large as a cave. He leaned farther out over the water, stretching his neck thin, elongating it like a snake's. He couldn't hold this position for long so he coiled himself under the towel and half-closed his eyes, making them hooded the way he imagined a cobra's would be. He felt sleepy.

For a long time he lay there, eyes hooded, imagining he was a snake. He saw himself lying on a dry, dusty slope. He saw a motorbike with a bubble-headed body coming towards him. He felt himself coil into a tight circle, his head swaying, ready to spring. The motorbike came close, closer. He saw a brown leg. He coiled himself tighter, then sprang against the leg. He felt his fangs go into flesh. He felt the shudder and fall of a body. Another motorbike came into view. It came close, closer. The leg on this one was fat and white. Quickly, before it could veer away, he sank his fangs into the flesh. Now two bodies writhed on the ground while beside them two machines buzzed in the dust like giant overturned flies. And he, King of Snakes, drew himself up and watched them from beneath hooded eyes. He was most feared, Lord of them all.

He felt a splash of water on his face. He blinked. It was Louie holding onto the raft with one hand and spraying water on him with the other. "Hey," Louie said. "The water's great. Aren't you coming in?"

Slowly Stephen uncoiled himself.

"Sure," he said. He jumped into the water. The coldness stung his sunburn. Side by side they swam out to the cove mouth, their bathing suits bobbing like bright beach balls on the lake's surface. Stephen flipped over on his back and floated. He looked at the pyramidal mountain, its peak arrowing up into the blue, cloudless sky. The cave eye had opened wide.

When he and Louie were back on the dock, Stephen said, "When can we go up to the cave?"

"After we eat. If we start early enough, we might have time to get up there."

"And we can see Angus on the way," Stephen said.

"Maybe," Louie said. It was a long way up to the cave.

Aunt Lise was dying wool in the kitchen and hanging it in bags on the clothesline to dry. She bought her wool carded and spun, but she preferred to do the dying herself. That was how she got such vibrant colours. The kitchen was hot and steamy.

"You boys can help me," she said. She looked so tired and cross that neither boy refused.

While Louie stirred the pots simmering on the stove, Stephen hung the bags of coloured wool outside to dry. The bags kept slipping off the clothesline, but he finally managed to get them pegged to the line.

When they were done, Aunt Lise sent them outside while she cleared out the kitchen. They sat on the step in the shade, their stomachs rumbling from hunger and dissatisfaction. Relief came when Aunt Lise announced she had two plates of macaroni and cheese waiting for them. After they had bolted this down with slices of buttered bread, she said, "That ought to hold you for a while," which the boys took to mean they were free again.

They ran down the hill, threw their towels into *The Explorer* and shoved off. They were well away from the dock before they felt that something was missing. Louie noticed it first.

"Our raft," he said. "It's gone."

Stephen cupped both hands around the visor of the golf cap and stared. The water where the raft had been was completely bare.

Louie rowed swiftly to the seam of green-blue water.

His father had anchored the raft by lowering buckets of cement onto the lake bottom and tying them to the raft with leftover clothesline wire. Louie looked into the water and saw that the wires had been cut.

"Sludge. Willard," he said. "They cut the wires and hid our raft someplace. We'd better find it." He steered the dory towards the closed end of the cove where Riley's campground was. "They can't have towed it far."

The campground was in a pine grove near the water. There were plank tables, benches, firepits, bird houses and Mrs Riley's geraniums bordering the dock in red. Mrs Riley put geraniums in anything that would hold soil: basins, tins, coffeepots, an old hat. She had even planted geraniums in *The Explorer* before it was *The Explorer*, before she had given it to Mad, who had patched a hole in its side, sanded it smooth and given it two coats of marine paint. Tied to the dock was Riley's motorboat. The campground was deserted: most of the tourists came on the weekend. Even Mrs Riley's battered Ford was absent: she had gone to the village.

Louie and Stephen rowed past the dock in

silence, their eyes trained on the small inlets of water captured from the cove by encroaching reeds. In the last inlet, where the lake ran through a culvert beneath the road, they found the raft. Louie examined the trailing wires.

"They've been cut, all right," he said. He handed the wires to Stephen. "You tow the raft while I row."

It was hard work rowing back. Louie gave it all his concentration.

Stephen was the one who noticed the motor-bikes twinned together at the end of Riley's dock, half hidden by geraniums. They'd been there all the time. Searching for the raft had been like seeing the woods but not the trees, Stephen thought.

"Stop rowing," he said.

Louie stopped, his face flushed from exertion.

Stephen pointed.

"Why don't we let the air out of the tires?" He felt bold saying this and pleased to have thought of it.

"That would show them, all right," Louie said. He made for the dock.

It took less than ten minutes. Taking turns with Louie's new jack-knife, they opened the valves and allowed the hissing air to escape. Stephen pushed the tip of the knife against one of the tires experimentally, to see how the rubber resisted it. He pushed hard, harder, testing the tire for strength. Abruptly the tire gave way: the metal

tip stuck into the rubber. He had to pull hard to
get it out. He could see the hole it had made. He
had thought rubber was tougher than that. The
air whooshed out and the tire went flat.

"Let's get out of here. Quick!" Louie said.
They'd gone a little further than he'd intended,
even though Sludge and Willard had it coming
to them. They towed the raft back to its place. It
took several tries diving underwater before they
managed to get the wires retied to the buckets
and they were free to head for the opposite side
of the lake.

Louie rowed out of the cove. He avoided the middle of the lake where the water was blackest and
steered along one side. Here the water was bot-
tle green. Graceful weeds grew up from the bottom in a forest of magical trees coming so close
to the water's surface that Stephen thought rowing over them was like being in a low-flying plane
that barely skimmed the tree-tops. With volcanic
swiftness, an old beaver lodge from previous gen-
erations of beavers rose to meet them from below,
then another and another until they reached the
mound of freshly cut poplar and dirt that was the
active beaver lodge. Louie lifted his oars; water
dripped into the lake like drops of green rain. Neither spoke. They waited, hoping to see a beaver.
Above, an osprey hovered on a current of hot air
like a feathered kite. The sun beat down on them.
The air was silent, heavy with the burden of wait-

ing, with the knowledge that the next move was Sludge and Willard's. They felt suspended on wires: puppets in their own mime.

They heard shouts from Riley's dock.

"They've found the tires," Louie said. He picked up the oars and began rowing. They still had some distance to go before they reached the opposite shore. The lake was a mile across, and they were only three-quarters of the way there.

Louie rowed strenuously. The oarlocks creaked. The old boat lumbered on as if every inch were painful. They had nearly reached the shore when they heard a whoop across the water. Soon there was the choke and splutter of a motorboat coming to life. It was from Riley's dock.

"Quick!" Louie said. "We'll hide the dory in the eel grass. If we're fast we can get into the woods before they see us."

Behind them a boat raced towards the mouth of the cove.

The lake's end was in the shadow of the mountain. There were no houses or cabins here — just thickly wooded shoreline. Along the shoreline was a battalion of giant trees with bent trunks, amputated branches, bark scarred by age and storm. These were the warrior trees, sentinels posted to guard the wilderness from the advance of civilization.

The Explorer had reached the shadow of these trees. It creaked and groaned as Louie nosed its prow into the eel grass.

Out on the lake Riley's motorboat surged through the water, spray winging up from its sides.

"Hurry! They're gaining!" Louie said. "Give me a hand with the boat."

They stepped into knee-high water, their bare feet sinking into the silty bottom. Mud oozed up between their toes. Tugging and shoving, they manoeuvred the dory through the eel grass and up the small stream that trickled out of the woods.

The motorboat had reached the middle of the lake.

Louie and Stephen pushed the red boat deeper until they were satisfied that it was well concealed. Louie noticed Angus's big green canoe tied to a nearby tree.

"Let's go!" he said. He ducked beneath the battalion of trees and dived into a sea of waist-high scrub, Stephen beside him. Together they waded through the willows.

Behind them the motor boat droned like an angry hornet. They plunged ahead, arms and legs thrashing.

Beyond the willows the land rose steeply in out-croppings of grey rock. At the top of this rugged slope, the land flattened into a plateau and the wilderness changed completely. It was as if, having broken through the battalion of trees, they were being led to an enchanted place. On the plateau was a forest of majestically tall cedar trees. These trees did not grow thickly. There were spaces between, shady clean avenues. The late afternoon sun shone between the interweavings of boughs, making patterns on the forest floor. There was a rich smell of cedar on the warm air. It had a hypnotic effect on them. For a few moments it made them forget their enemies, forget that they were being pursued.

Louie sat down on a rock patterned with grey lace. The moss had white star-flowers growing from it. He thought of scraping some of the moss off to take back to his tree-lab because he had never seen it growing anywhere else, but there was something about this place that made him want to leave it here. He had the feeling that it would disappear if he took it away.

Stephen looked up at the tall cedars, at the green heads swaying at the tops of the giant trunks. He heard a sighing sound and wondered if the trees were visiting each other up there, nodding their heads together as the old people in Two Pine, the senior citizens' lodge where his grandmother lived, sometimes did, or whether they visited each other below the ground where their roots were entwined. His eyes travelled up the tree trunks.

And then he saw it.

Dangling in front of him was a face. A divided face that was half black and half red and edged with trailing wisps of hair. The face had round holes for eyes, a broken splayed nose and a mouth twisted into a grimace that was half pleasure, half pain. There was no body to this head, only the face staring at him between the trees. The eye holes held Stephen fast, rooted him to the spot. Without moving the rest of his body, he opened his mouth.

"Louie," he croaked. "What's that?"

Louie laughed. "It's a mask, you dummy. It must be new. I've never seen it before." He paused. "I wonder if it's the one Mrs Riley saw Old Angus wearing last night."

He walked over to the mask and twirled it around, admiring it. The mask was tied onto a branch with a heavy rope knotted through a hole in its head.

There was the sound of a boat's motor being cut, shouts from the bottom of the slope.

"They're here," Louie said. "The cave'll have to wait. We'd better hide." Louie knew better than to break a fresh trail through the woods, a trail that could be easily followed. Out here in the wilderness who knew what those bullies would do? He led the way into a forest of masks. Here the woods opened up like a courtyard, its floor springy with moss. In the middle of the floor were flat stones arranged in circles and lines. There were tall cedar columns on either side. Hanging from the branches were more wooden masks. Some of the faces were human and some animal. Some had smooth cheeks, sunken mouths, straight noses, blank eyes; others had angular snouts, foreheads deeply scored, twisted lips. All of them had hair: trailing wisps of Spanish moss, fur tufts, dried grass, feathers, horns. And each mask was boldly painted in red, green, black, brown, yellow, white, blue.

The shouts came nearer.

"Quick!" Louie said. "Put a mask on."

A few of the masks were low enough for them to reach. Using his jack-knife, Louie cut down a coyote mask and put it on.

By standing on a stump, Stephen got his face behind a bear mask which was tied to a low branch. The mask was brown. It had a hooked nose, a wide red mouth, square teeth and eye-holes ringed with yellow. There were thin strips of hide at the sides to keep the mask in place. Stephen tied the strips behind his head. The inside of the mask was dark and smelled of new cedar. He breathed in deeply, then hunched forward, bearlike. His skin tingled as if it were being pricked by hundreds of tiny fur spines. His feet and hands itched; his ears twitched. He heard someone yelling close by. He peered through the small eye holes and saw two boys walking into the courtyard. He didn't like the look of either of them. One was a fat boy with round cheeks and a phony smile on his face. The other was taller and thinner with shrewd eyes that darted quickly from mask to mask.

Willard pointed at Stephen, then leaped towards him. Stephen roared through his bear mouth. Willard stumbled backwards and fell against Sludge.

"Watch what you're doing," Sludge whined. Something sharp poked him in the back. He yelped and turned around. Peering at him from behind a tree was a face that was half man, half beast. It had pricked-up ears, a sharp nose and a crooked grin. It waved a clawed stick at his face.

Willard made a lunge for the stick and tripped over a tree root. With a ghoulish wail, Coyote pounced on the fallen body and began pummelling the arms and chest with the stick.

"Get him off me, Sludge!"

Sludge circled the masked figure sitting on Willard's stomach but was beaten off by Coyote. The claw stick raked his chin. Sludge gave Coyote a shove.

Seeing this, Bear tried to get off the stump, but having no knife he was unable to cut the rope. Had it not been tied to the top of his head, he might have chewed himself free. As it was, all he could do was prance up and down on the stump. One claw raked the tree trunk beside him; the other pawed the air. His head rocked from side to side.

Sludge looked at him fearfully. "Bears rear up like that when they're mad. He's coming to get us. Let's get out of here!"

Sludge and Willard turned tail and ran out of the forest. Behind them Coyote howled with laughter. Then he sprang to the stump where Bear was rocking. With one thrust of the knife he set Bear free.

Bear lowered his front paws and jumped down. He lifted his head and growled, his voice rumbling furiously. He padded in a wide circle around the clearing, roaring and growling. Behind him Coyote leaped and howled, his claw stick flailing the air. He began to laugh high and shrill, tapping the stick on Bear's back. Bear swung around, swiped the stick from Coyote and threw it on the ground. Growling, Bear rose up on his hind legs and danced. Moving backwards, Coyote partnered this dance. Round and round they danced, circling and recircling, the dance becoming faster and faster, charged with a wild, primitive frenzy. Abruptly they broke off dancing. Bear began to hit the trees, ramming his head against the thick trunks. Coyote swung from low branches and, with his feet, broke off bits of cedar and bark. Then, with a howling war whoop, he flung himself onto Bear's back and pounded on him with his paws.

"That's enough!" a loud voice resounded through the forest.

And the boys felt their masks slipping away.

Five

Stephen found himself in front of the tallest man he'd ever seen, a man at least seven feet tall, a giant with a dark, angry face and a white pigtail down his back. The man was wearing moccasins and a deerskin jacket. The masks dangled from his hands like severed heads.

"This isn't a place of war," he roared. "There is no fighting on sacred ground."

"We were only fooling around," Louie said.

"You were meddling with evil spirits," the voice boomed.

Far up the mountain Stephen heard a rumbling sound, the beginning of a rockslide.

"What evil spirits?" Louie said carelessly. He

had been over here before with his parents; he wasn't afraid of Old Angus.

Stephen was amazed at his boldness.

The giant was getting angrier.

"Do you want to awaken the Wild Man of the Woods?" he roared.

There was another rumble as more rocks tumbled down.

Stephen felt like running away, but Louie stood his ground.

"I don't even know who the Wild Man of the Woods is," he said. "And certainly I didn't know this was sacred ground."

Old Angus looked up the mountain and back again. It was a quick, furtive look, as if he felt he was being watched. Then he said, in a low, toneless voice, "The Wild Man of the Woods is an evil mask." He waited until the rocks had slid to a standstill; then he went on. "The stones can tell you about the sacredness of this ground."

Angus reached up and tied the masks to the trees. Then he pointed to the stones. "Do you see them?"

Though the deep voice was gentler now, Stephen felt it was still big enough to be inside two people. He walked over to the stones.

"Those are markers made by my people," Angus said. "They used to camp here waiting for the elk herds to come down from the high valleys."

Louie strolled over for a closer look at the

stones. They were arranged in two circles, one smaller than the other. There were short pebbled lines coming out from the larger circle.

"It's a body," Louie said. It looked like the crude stick figures he used to draw when he was a little kid, a head and a belly.

Stephen stood where he was. He was afraid of this giant. He was thinking that the man didn't look old. He had white hair, all right, and his face was as deeply grooved as wet bark, but he wasn't stooped and frail like their grandmother, Marie Delphine. He stood tall and cedar straight.

"That is the body of Crooked Beak," Angus said.

"Who was he?" Louie said carelessly, only half interested. He didn't want to be told a lot of school stuff about Indians, but his curiosity led him on.

"A young man who was killed here many years ago."

This sounded more interesting.

"How was he killed?" Louie said.

Angus spread his long body on the ground. Stephen noticed that both his feet and his head touched edges of the clearing.

"In a war," Angus said.

"What war?"

"A war between himself and another man."

"You can't have war between two people," Louie protested.

"Do you want to hear about him or not?" Angus said.

"Go ahead," Louie said. He wasn't in that big a hurry to leave these woods. Willard and Sludge might be lurking in the trees, waiting for them.

"Crooked Beak wasn't from here but from a tribe who lived in a valley across the lake. It was said that as a baby he'd been crushed by a large rock so that he grew up broken nosed and limp legged. Because he was small and quick, he was sent out to scout for food. Often he was seen scuttling through the woods over here like a crab on the sea bottom, but he always got away before anyone could grab him. Until one cold winter day, when a young man named Bighand was left behind with the women and children to guard camp while the other men went off to hunt elk. Bighand was hunched down in front of the fire, and Crooked Beak crept up behind him."

Angus rolled onto his belly and rubbed a large hand over one of the smooth stones.

For a man not given to words, Stephen thought, Angus was sure talking a lot.

"Maybe the two men could have been friends. Both were new to their manhood, eager to prove themselves," he continued. "But they were enemies. For years their tribes had been quarrelling over hunting territories. There was never enough food for everyone."

Angus's eyes clouded over as if he could see Bighand sitting in front of the fire and the other man creeping up behind him.

"Bighand heard a twig crack. He turned around

and saw Crooked Beak crouched down with a
knife. Because they were enemies, that knife
wasn't seen as a tool but as a weapon. Bighand
reached out to knock the knife to the ground, but
instead he knocked over Crooked Beak. Crooked
Beak hit his head on this stone and died.''

Louie waited for Angus to say more.

''Is that all?'' he said.

It didn't sound like much of a war to him.

''The men returned from the hunt with nothing. They blamed their empty bellies on Crooked
Beak and his people. It was a bad winter. No food.
Many babies died. There was more fighting. War
spreads like fire, especially when hunger feeds
it. So it went, year after year, until the people
who lived here either died or moved away.''

''What happened to Bighand?''

''He was sent away,'' Angus said, his voice bit-
ter and sad. ''When he returned many years later,
there was nothing here but these stones.''

While Angus talked, Stephen was staring at the
big man's feet, which were so tightly laced into
moccasins that each toe was clearly outlined. He
was thinking that they were the same size as the
footprints he had seen on the lake bottom.

''I still don't see why this is sacred ground,''
Louie said.

Angus closed his eyes. Louie watched his face
for an answer, but the only sound he heard was
the sighing of trees.

Finally Angus said, ''Crooked Beak didn't have

to die. Remembering that is a way of keeping the peace.''

There was the sound of a boat motor trying to come alive. It coughed, spluttered, caught for a brief moment, then died.

Stephen's gaze wandered across the masks hanging in the trees. He stared at the twisted, broken noses, the crooked, snaggle-toothed mouths, the scars deeply scoring the cheeks and foreheads.

''Why have you made these faces so ugly?'' he suddenly burst out. ''People aren't *that* ugly.''

''Do you mean inside or out?'' Angus smiled. His eyes were still closed so that Stephen didn't see that he was half teasing.

Stephen thought of his nightmares.

''They sure are scary,'' he said.

''They have to be to drive away evil spirits,'' Angus said.

This time the boat motor caught, humming louder and louder until at last it was heading across the lake.

''What evil spirits?'' Louie said impatiently. His father never talked about evil spirits. A wooden spoon was just a wooden spoon. ''Where are these spirits?''

''Everywhere,'' Angus said. He opened his eyes and looked at Louie. ''You don't believe,'' he said. ''I'll show you.'' He got up and walked out of the clearing. In ten strides he was through the woods and into another clearing, Louie and

Stephen hopping like small birds after him. In this clearing there was a huge teepee with stars, moons, suns painted on its sides. In front of the teepee on the cedar chip carpeting was a firepit and a work table made of long planks mounted on wooden horses. On the table were chisels, knives, mallets, brushes and paint, and next to it was a large stool.

"Do you know how I carve my masks?" Angus said. He picked up a mallet and chisel and went back into the woods.

Louie grimaced. Watching someone carve was nothing new to him. He had been hoping for something else. But Stephen was eagerly following the big man through the trees, so Louie had no choice but to go along.

They went some distance before Angus stopped in front of a large cedar from which a large square of bark had been peeled away. On the naked red surface was the ghost of a face. By squinching up his eyes Stephen could see the beginnings of a mask. It seemed to be a rounded face with a whistling mouth and full cheeks, but in the sun-dappled shade it was difficult to see.

Gently Angus eased the chisel into place where the mouth seemed to be.

Stephen felt a cool breeze against the damp hair of his temples.

"The wind spirit is in this tree," Angus said. "You see, everything in the forest has a spirit, even the smallest stones. At night when I am sleeping these spirits appear, begging me to give them a face." Angus thrust the chisel deeper. "And I do."

"How do you do that?" Louie said.

"I dream. I walk. I fast."

It was clear Angus carved in a different way from his father, who, if anything, ate more when he was carving, not less.

"But why do they want to get out?"

"Everything wants to be free. Nothing should be locked up."

Stephen noticed that the big hands trembled slightly. But they were not the hands of an old man. The brown fingers were long and supple. They looked as if they could crush a skull or tear up a young sapling.

"Why do you wear your masks?" he said. "Mrs Riley said you frightened her out of her wits."

Angus smiled. "Mrs Riley frightens easy. I didn't think anyone would see me out there on the lake. I often go out in the canoe after dark. That night I just finished a mask and I wanted to put it on. I like to feel its power."

"What about the Wild Man of the Woods?" Louie said. "Have you ever put it on?"

The chisel slid from Angus's hand. Louie picked it up and handed it back to him. The old man snatched it angrily. When he spoke again his voice was harsh. "The Wild Man of the Woods is not one of my masks. It is an ugly, evil mask."

"Where did it come from?"

"It probably began in the same way as children's fairytales. People thought Wild Man was a ghost who lured them away by offering his food. If someone ate it, he became a ghost like Wild Man. It was harmless enough. Then someone came along who could not be satisfied with this. He saw evil where others had not. He carved a fierce, ugly mask that filled people with such terror they were afraid to go into the woods."

"Maybe it was a shaman or a medicine man, somebody like that," Stephen suggested.

"The people banded together and drove the evil carver to a cave up the mountain. They used to say he could be seen roaming the woods near the cave, but that was a long time ago. He's dead now."

"But his mask must still be there," Louie persisted.

"Yes, and there it will stay." Angus stabbed the chisel into the tree with finality.

A sudden gust of wind pushed roughly against the tree-tops. The giant cedars groaned to their root-tips. The boys stood in the darkening light watching the face of the wind emerge.

Until they heard the faint ring of a bell echoing across the lake.

"My parents," Louie said. "We'd better go."

They left the clearing.

"Just as well we didn't go up to the cave," Louie said when they were out of earshot.

"Are you sure it's the same cave?"

"No, but it probably is. There aren't any others around here that I know of."

They entered the woods. Yellow rays of late sun slanted through green branches, holding them in a timeless quietude as if they were swimming underwater. They walked through the forest of masks, where masks bright as tropical fish twirled in the breeze. They came to the edge of the plateau, slid down the rock outcropping, plunged into the sea of willows, then ducked beneath the sentinel firs and came to the eel grass where they had left *The Explorer*.

Louie was first to see the patch of broken red. But it wasn't until he was beside the dory that he saw the hole gouged in her prow. It was the same hole Mad had painstakingly repaired with a plywood square and fibreglass. Now it had reopened like an ugly wound that would not heal.

Louie looked across the darkening lake.

"Sludge and Willard," he said. "They did this."

Stephen stared at the hole: it looked as if it had been kicked in, or perhaps one of the oars had been used to do the job.

"Get in," Louie said. "I'll row. You bail. Sit as close as you can to the centre."

Although *The Explorer* sat low in the water, the hole was high enough on one side so that when Stephen sat in the centre, the waterline was below the opening. Stephen picked up the plastic detergent container Mad had cut into a bailing scoop.

Louie pushed off and got in. The dory wobbled, and water leaked into the hole.

"Sit still," he commanded and picked up the oars. "And keep an eye on the hole." He had his back to the prow.

To save time they rowed across the middle, which shone sleek and black as oil. A breeze riffled the lake surface and the hair on Stephen's neck. Small waves slopped through the hole. He leaned forward — carefully, so as not to wobble the boat — and bailed. He was sitting in an inch of water.

"Bail harder!" Louie yelled. It did not seem to him that his cousin was working as hard as he should. He was the one with the more difficult job. Already his shoulders were sore from rowing, and they weren't half-way there. He was worrying about what Mad would say when she saw the hole. She had loaned him the dory on the condition that he take good care of it. Would she believe it wasn't his fault, that Willard and Sludge were mean enough to wreck her boat? She didn't have the same problem with those jerks. He'd be in trouble with his parents, too, for coming home so late. Louie set his jaw and rowed harder. *The Explorer* jerked forward like an injured whale.

They stopped at the beaver lodge to rest. Both were too tired to look for the beaver. From here Louie could see their dock. There was a figure on it, someone sitting in a lawn chair. His father.

Louie waved. His father waved back and rang the cowbell. He had brought it down to the dock, a bad sign.

Stephen put down the bailer; his shoulders were sore where his sunburn was worst.

"Want me to row now?" he said.

"No, I'd better do it," Louie said. He was in enough trouble as it was, and Mad might not want anyone except him rowing the dory.

He rowed on in silence punctuated only by the creak of oarlocks and the swish and plop of Stephen's bailing.

At last they reached shore. Louie's father met them at the end of the dock.

"What happened?" he said, looking at the hole.

The boys clambered onto the dock.

"An accident. The boat got jammed against a rock," Louie said tersely. He glared at Stephen, defying him to offer a contradiction.

But Stephen kept his eyes down, allowing Louie to handle the lie. He heard his uncle say, "A strange thing to have happened. Up so high on the prow like that. Where was this rock?"

"On the other side of the lake there's a huge rock on the shore where we pulled in the boat. It's real sharp."

"It must have been."

Stephen did not see the quizzical expression on his uncle's face, because when he lifted his eyes the lie was over and his uncle was saying,

"Well you'd better come up to the house. Your
mother's been worried. You shouldn't go off for
so long without telling us where you're going.
We'll patch up that hole in the morning."

Aunt Lise had warm rolls and cold salad waiting for them. The salad had devilled eggs in
it, and there was real butter for the rolls. They
wolfed down the food, scarcely noticing that the
chameleon sky was slowly camouflaging itself
with night.

After they had eaten, they went upstairs and
tumbled wearily into their bunks. Before closing
his eyes, Stephen looked at the prone body on
the opposite bunk.

"Why didn't you tell your father the truth?"
he said.

"And have him go over to Mrs Riley?" Louie
said. "That would make it worse." He pulled the
sheet up over his head and mumbled sleepily,
"We have to handle this ourselves."

Stephen pulled up his sheet, blocking out the
light. He was pleased that Louie had said *we* and
ourselves. Being included this way made Stephen
feel strong and aggressive. Now that he had an
ally, he would learn to fight at last.

Six

*I*n the morning Stephen awoke early. He got up and looked out the window. Through the trees he saw a thick white cloud suspended over the lake. The mountain appeared to be poking up through it, the peak rose gold in the rising sun.

"Come and get it," his uncle called from the kitchen.

Stephen and Louie got into their clothes and hurried downstairs. Aunt Lise, who had been up late weaving, was sleeping in. Uncle Adam was cooking bacon at the stove. Stephen heard the fire beneath the pan crackling and spitting. Coffee steamed in the pot. Beside it, oatmeal bubbled, its surface lifting in small geysers.

After breakfast Uncle Adam sent Louie to the

workshop for a square of plywood, screws, glue
and tools. The three of them went down to the
dock to work on *The Explorer*. They tipped the
dory on her side, pouring out the swill, then lifted
her onto the dock. The hole was ragged with
splinters. They pulled these away; then Uncle
Adam knelt down and sanded the edges smooth.
Louie made a neat border of glue on the plywood
square, then held it in place while his father
screwed the square over the hole. While they
worked, a red-winged blackbird teased them from
her perch on a bulrush, trying to distract them
from her nest. She sounded like the whirr of a
party favour being unfurled.

"There. That ought to do it," Uncle Adam said
and stood up. "Give it a couple of hours to dry,
and then you can cut a square of fibreglass and
seal it on with Varathane."

"Could we paint it today?" Louie didn't like
the bare spot against the expanse of red wood.

"No, not until tomorrow. Right now I want you
to keep an eye on the shop. I have to go to the
lumber yard for two-by-fours to make our fair
stall."

Stephen was reluctant to leave the dock. He
could tell it was going to be a hot day. Already
the cloud had burned off the centre of the lake,
but here in the cove it was shady and cool. Before
the heat came he wanted to bask in the quiet rest-
fulness. Even Riley's campground was silent. But
Louie had already picked up the tools and was

walking up the hill with his father. Stephen ran to catch up.

After his father had driven away, Louie printed RING BELL FOR SERVICE on a board with the red crayon and propped it against the shop door. He went into the living room and came back with the cowbell. He hung this on the door above the sign.

"Let's go into the workshop," he said. "We can hear anyone who comes from there. I feel like making something."

"What?"

"You'll see."

They entered by the outside screen door. The workshop was green and cool, like a room in the woods made from woven boughs.

Louie went to the space beneath the stairs and snapped on the light cord. "We're allowed to use any of this stuff we want," he said. He bent over and yanked out a long strip of fir. The wood was narrow and smooth. Louie tested it for strength.

"Should make a good spear," he said.

He took it to the work-bench. Stephen selected a smooth triangle of wood and three smaller chunks. He took these to the work-bench and nailed the smaller pieces onto one side of the triangle to make a handle. He sanded the edges.

"You got any paints?" he said.

"In the cupboard by the wall," Louie said. He was carving the tip of his spear into a sharp arrowhead.

Stephen found red and yellow paint. He wanted colours that were bright and bold. A shield should look ugly and fierce.

They heard a car drive up, then the cowbell being rung. Louie put down his spear and went upstairs. While he was gone, Stephen carefully outlined eyes, nose and mouth, then made bold designs on the forehead and cheeks, painting it like a warrior's face. The face had to be strong enough to attack and at the same time defend. He propped it up on the work-bench to admire its fierce ugliness.

Louie came back. "Lookers, not buyers," he said. He picked up his spear.

Stephen went back to the wood supply and selected two stout pieces of fir, shorter than Louie's but sturdier. The edges of one were sharp enough for a blade. Stephen nailed the other piece crosswise to make a sword. When that was done, he sanded the edges while Louie finished his spear. When they heard Aunt Lise moving about upstairs, they carried their weapons down to the tree-lab. Then they checked the dory.

"The glue's set. It's time to put on the fibre-glass," Louie said.

While Louie ran back for materials, Stephen sat on the dock beside the boat and looked at the lake. The cove was now in full sunlight, winking like a yellow-green jewel. From next door he heard the thwack of an axe, the soft thud of wood falling on the ground.

Soon Louie was back. Working together they covered the wooden patch with fibreglass and sealed the edges. Stephen gophered up the ladder, stowed the materials in the tree-lab and came back down with the weapons.

"C'mon," Louie said. "Let's find Sludge and Willard."

Crouched over, they crept into the bushes and beneath their barbed wire fence. Louie kept his spear low so it wouldn't stick out through the branches. Stephen hugged his shield close. They inched forward until they had a view of the campground through the leaves. In front of a small shingled house Mrs Riley was chopping wood. Her face was red and shiny with perspiration. She had a kerchief tied over her black hair. With each lift of her arms the bulk beneath her print dress shifted, and her earrings swung to and fro. Mrs Riley paused to rest, wiping her damp forehead with her kerchief. She glanced in their direction, but she didn't see them.

Watching Mrs Riley chop kindling reminded Louie that the old lady had once given him wood and several glass jars for his tree-lab. He had the sudden urge to forget Sludge and Willard, to walk over there, take the axe from her and say in a big, manly voice: *Here, let me do that for you.* But the moment passed as quickly as it had come. He had no intention of doing Sludge's work for him.

"Sludge is probably over at Soper's. C'mon. Let's go."

The Sopers lived on the other side of the road, past the culvert where the lake drained into a swamp. The boys emerged from the bushes and walked boldly across the slope to the road. But they avoided Soper's gravel driveway, making their approach by way of the swamp instead. There were bulrushes to provide cover, so they were able to get close without being seen.

The trailer where Willard lived with his father and mother was in a rough clearing where tree stumps had been left to weather grey. There was a TV aerial on top of the trailer and a road-weary truck outside. Leaning against the truck was Willard's motorbike. A much larger truck with Ace Transport on its side was parked farther down the driveway. The yard was strewn with rusted metal scraps and piles of wood overgrown with weeds. Sludge and Willard were sitting on the running-board. Willard was loading a gun.

Stephen drew his shield closer.

"Are those real bullets?" he whispered.

"Yeah. It's a twenty-two," Louie whispered back. "His father lets him use it for target practice if he's around. But once I saw Willard take it out to the beaver dam when he was by himself."

"Why'd he take it out there?"

"To use on the beaver, I guess. Keep down."

Willard stood up. He went to the garbage can beside the trailer and fished out an empty soup can. He handed it to Sludge.

''Put it on top of the stump under the clothes-line,'' he said.

Obediently Sludge set the can on the stump, which was between the trailer and the black sedan.

Willard backed up, lifted the gun and fired. There was a dull crack as the bullet hit a tree behind the stump.

Stephen saw a smirk form on Sludge's mouth, but it was quickly wiped away.

Willard cursed and fired once more. Again he missed. He lifted the gun and tried again. There was a loud ping as the bullet bounced off the trailer.

''What the hell d'you think you're doin' out there?'' a voice bellowed.

A man stepped off the flimsy step. He was short and barrel chested, with a bull neck and thick shoulders.

''Is that Mr Soper?'' Stephen whispered.

Louie nodded.

''Willard sure doesn't look like his old man.''

Willard hung his head.

''He looks like his mother,'' Louie whispered.

''Why don't you hold the thing the way I showed you?'' His father took the gun away from Willard, took aim and fired.

The soup can jumped off the stump.

''Like that.'' His father shoved the gun at Willard.

Sludge put the soup can back on the stump.

Willard took aim, fired. He hit the tree behind the stump.

"How the hell am I gonna take you huntin' if you can't hit a tin can from twenty feet, eh?" his father yelled. Once again he took the gun. "Now watch what I do. Remember, you gotta keep your eye on the target." Mr Soper aimed and fired. Once again the soup can jumped off the stump. "Nothing to it." He handed the gun to Willard.

But Willard shook his head.

"Don't be stupid," his father said. When Willard refused to take the gun, his father shrugged. "Have it your way," he said and took the gun inside.

Within moments he was at the door, bellowing through the screen. "You want that tire of yours fixed for the parade tomorrow, you better get it onto the truck. I gotta go in for your mother's pills."

Willard and Sludge wrestled the motorbike onto the back of the truck and climbed up after it. Mr Soper came out and got in the truck, and they drove away. The truck had no muffler and sounded like an army tank.

Louie and Stephen emerged from the bulrushes. Louie walked over and picked up the soup can. It had two holes blasted through the middle.

"I know how we can get even," he whispered. They had to be careful. Mrs Soper was inside watching the soaps. He could hear the TV.

"How?"

"Rig up a dummy and set it on the stump. Maybe those dummies will get the message."

They used the legs Louie had cut off his jeans. They stuffed the dummy with bits of cloth from Aunt Lise's rag bag. For arms and face they used an old pair of nylons. Stephen sewed on buttons to make the eyes, nose and mouth. He found some brown wool and sewed it on for hair, tufting it up like Willard's. Louie pulled on one of his old shirts to make a torso. They worked quickly, wanting to get the job done before the enemy returned. When they were done they carried the dummy across the road and up Soper's driveway. The TV was still on. Stealthily they crept across the yard and set the dummy on the stump where the soup can had been. But the dummy wouldn't sit straight: it kept sliding onto the ground.

Stephen spied the rope clothesline.

"Let's string it up," he whispered. While Louie watched the trailer door in case Mrs Soper should appear, Stephen untied the rope. He secured one end around the dummy's neck; the other he threw over a branch and tied to a nearby tree. The dummy dangled over the stump, swaying like the corpse of a hanged man.

They heard the truck gunning up the driveway.

"They're back!" Louie whispered.

They ran for cover in the swamp, crawling over clumps of last year's bulrushes.

The truck blasted to a stop in front of the trailer.

Louie and Stephen dashed across the road.

"Head for the tree-lab!" Louie said.

They clambered up the ladder, opened the door and flopped inside. They lay on the cool boards and waited, but there was no sign of Willard or Sludge.

Hunger finally drove them uphill to the log house. No one was in the kitchen, so they made themselves a snack of Cheez Whiz and crackers. Louie found some leftover lemonade and they drank that. Downstairs they heard the sound of hammering and, from the studio, the clack of Aunt Lise's loom as she swung the shuttle back and forth. They wandered into the living-room. Louie picked up his comics. Stephen saw the book *Great Masks* lying on the table. He put it on his knees and began to turn the pages. There were pictures of masks from all over the world. One was an African king mask with ringed ears and a headpiece that fanned out like a lion's mane. Another was a chalk-white Greek mask with a tragic, gaping mouth. Stephen wondered if his father had come across one of these in his travels. There was a South American carnival mask with garish painted features and a Mexican stone mask smoothed by wind and rain. Stephen kept turning pages. He came to a mask of white plaster. It looked like a real face. It was the death mask of an old man. Beneath it was an inscription: "Give a man a mask, and he will tell the truth." Stephen turned the page, then flipped it back and reread the words, fascinated because he didn't know what they meant. *What* truth did they mean? The truth about the person himself, or did the mask have a truth of its own? He passed a Pharoah's golden tomb mask and came to Canadian Indian masks. There was one of a thunderbird and another of an eagle. Both were brightly painted like the sun mask. Louie looked up at the giver of life. Sun angled through the window of the loft and fell on the red and yellow face, firing it to a pulsing orange. He looked at the masks in the book. None, he thought, was as beautiful as the mask on the wall.

Stephen turned another page and quickly slammed his hand down flat. He had just come to the ugliest mask he'd ever seen. It had a bulging greenish black head, small red eyes, jagged triangular teeth and snake hair. The face stared at him through fingers splayed like bars across the page. Slowly Stephen lifted his hand. Beneath the picture he read, "The Wild Man of the Woods —a cannibal mask."

Stephen dropped the book as though it had just caught fire.

"Louie," he said. "Come here. There's something in this book you should see."

"Huh?" Louie went on reading: the Superheroes were closing in.

Gingerly Stephen picked up the book and eased it onto the table. With one finger he flicked the pages until he came to the horrible mask.

"Look!" he pointed.

Louie leaned sideways over the chair for a quick glance, then jerked backward.

"Holy crow. That's it! That's the Wild Man of the Woods!"

"That's it, all right." Stephen walked to the window and gazed over the lake.

Low on the mountain he saw the cave, a dark eye staring at him.

Louie whistled softly. "It's a cannibal mask. Angus didn't tell us that."

Stephen couldn't take his eyes off the cave. Louie came to stand beside him. Stephen noticed a tall black tree that stuck up out of the wilderness like a spike. He had never noticed it before. It looked like the eye of the cave was snagged on top of that tree.

"What's that tree?" he said.

"Dad calls it a compass tree," Louie said. "He says it's so big, towering over the other trees like it does, that you could use it to keep from getting lost."

"Ever been up to it?"

"Not yet."

After a while Louie said, "Do you think it's the same mask Angus was talking about?"

"Could be," Stephen said slowly. "Or could

be there's more than one Wild Man of the Woods.''

Louie went back and stared at the picture again.

''We should go up to the cave, see if it's the same one,'' he said excitedly. ''It can't be two places at once, can it?''

''Maybe it's in different countries under different names. Masks are everywhere.''

Suddenly Stephen felt surrounded by masks. The reflection of his own face stared back at him from the window, cold and unfamiliar. He turned and saw Louie's snub-nosed profile and shaggy black hair. That face could belong to lots of people. He looked at the mountain. It, too, had a face, the face of a sharp-featured, one-eyed man with deeply fissured skin. The mountain face looked tired, as if all its energy were being focussed into that one eye. Stephen felt himself being sucked into the eye hole.

''We should go up soon,'' he said. But the words were no sooner out of his mouth than he reached out and slammed the book shut.

Seven

''I've got a job for you two,'' Uncle Adam called to them. He had come upstairs to make himself a cup of tea.

''Another one?'' Louie grumbled.

Reluctantly the boys followed him downstairs.

Uncle Adam had built a wooden fair stall. It was a three-sided cubicle made of plywood sheets hinged together.

''I want you to stain the plywood. Lise's weavings will show up better against dark wood.'' He handed Louie a paintbrush and a tin of stain. ''Brush it on evenly. Stephen, you rub it in with rags.''

As newcomers to the valley, the Barrows had waited three years before being invited to display their crafts at the local fair. They were eager to do a good job of it.

Louie painted a wide swath of stain across the back panel.

"Follow the grain," his father advised.

Stephen rubbed in the stain. Beneath his rag the wood became the colour of maple syrup.

"Good," Uncle Adam said. He got a large cardboard box, and wrapping each carving in newspaper, he carefully stowed it inside. There were a pair of book-ends, a large salad bowl with six smaller bowls nesting inside, a small wooden chest, a pepper-mill, the snake spoon and the pair of matching lamps.

When the carvings were packed and the panels stained, the boys went upstairs to wash their hands. Aunt Lise was in the kitchen ironing placemats. She had already ironed three aprons, a tablecloth, a set of napkins, a shawl and two skirts, which were spread on the table. The table looked as if it had been strewn with flowers.

"Louie, do you have any more pressed butterflies?" she said.

"I have four," Louie said.

"That'll do," Aunt Lise said. "After supper I'd like you to get them. I'm going to decorate the shades for your father's lamps tonight."

While Aunt Lise finished her ironing, Stephen poured milk, Louie made toast and Uncle Adam scrambled eggs. When the food was ready they carried their toast and eggs into the living-room and sat on scattered chairs to eat, balancing their plates on their knees. High on the wall the mask glowed, reddened by the setting sun, enveloping them in a warm feeling of peace.

Afterwards Uncle Adam did the dishes while Aunt Lise packed her weavings. The boys took their time sauntering down to the tree-lab. Louie climbed up the ladder to the tree-house.

Stephen heard the padlock snap and the door open. He saw Louie crawl inside. Then he heard. "OUCH! I cut myself!" He watched, puzzled, as Louie stood up and covered his eyes. "Oh no!" Louie moaned.

Stephen went quickly up the ladder and stuck his head inside. He blinked into the gloom and shook his head, disbelieving.

The floor of the tree-house was littered with broken glass and puddled water. A moth floundered half alive in one of the puddles. Two water spiders with splayed legs were stranded on a dry patch of floor. Birds' eggs, cocoons, grasshoppers and caterpillars had been squashed together into a slimy jam. The frog was frozen in a dark corner, its throat ballooned out in fear as the garter-snake slithered towards it. Beneath a window the dummy was skewered to the wall with the crossed spear and sword. The shield lay on the floor, its painted face smeared into ugly blotches.

For a long time neither boy spoke. Louie stood there sucking his cut thumb.

Finally Stephen said, "They must've come

through the window.'' He put the terrified frog in an unbroken jar. He looked at the four dead butterflies pressed between the panes of glass.

"At least the monarchs are all right,'' he said.

But Louie seemed not to have heard. He stared moodily into the trees.

"Don't feel too bad,'' Stephen said briskly. "We'll get even with them.'' He felt strong being the leader. He thought of the mask in the cave.

"Why don't we ask your parents if we can camp on the other side of the lake?'' he said. "That way we can get up to the cave first thing in the morning.''

Louie was silent.

"We'd better go,'' Stephen said. "Your mother will be waiting for these.'' He lifted the panes of glass and Louie removed the butterflies. Stephen carried the frog jar and the snake down the ladder.

"You look like you've seen a ghost,'' Aunt Lise said when they walked into the kitchen.

Louie walked past his mother and went upstairs to the loft.

"He's tired,'' Stephen explained.

"Just as well he's gone to bed,'' Aunt Lise said. "We want you boys to help us at the fair tomorrow. It'll be a long day.''

Stephen felt disappointment thudding inside him. They would have to wait another day before going up to the cave.

"Could Louie and me camp across the lake sometime soon?'' he said.

"Once the fair is over I don't see why not,''

Aunt Lise said. She bent over the butterflies. "These are perfect specimens." She had already pinned Mrs Riley's pressed flowers onto a lampshade. She added the monarchs. When she finished arranging them to her satisfaction, she began to glue them down.

Stephen went downstairs and found an empty shoe box under his uncle's work-bench. He poked air holes in the cardboard and put the snake inside. Then he carried the box and the jar upstairs to the loft. Louie was already in bed, the sheet over his face. Stephen looked out the window. The evening sky was deep mauve. It was not dark enough for stars. The moon had not yet risen. The mountain was heavily shadowed, its back to the sun. The lake had a fallen look, as if its bottom had opened and the water were draining away.

Stephen put the snake box near the window weighing the top down with *Mysteries From Outer Space*. He unscrewed the top of the jar and set the jar on its side so the frog could get out. Then he undressed and got into bed. He tried to stay awake so he could see the moon when it rose. But his eyelids refused to stay open.

He was asleep when he saw the moon. He and Louie were up in the tree-lab. Except for the window of the moon it was pitch dark. They were wearing white space uniforms. All of the walls were made of bullet-proof glass: even the floor was glass. Mounted in the centre of the lab was a steel structure that shone coldly in the moonlight. *Poised on the top of this structure, ready to be fired, was a long missile, its nose needle sharp. Outside the lab, in the trees, were two boys. They were dangling by their collars from meat hooks dug into the branches; their hands were tied behind their backs.*

"Ready to load," Stephen said.

Louie pressed a button.

A glass wall slid open.

The hanging bodies swung inside on their hooks. The wall slid shut.

"Strap them in position." Stephen's orders were gruff and terse.

"Aye, aye, Captain." Louie pushed a second button. The hooks dropped their load onto the missile like two chunks of meat. Louie buckled the bodies into place so they were sitting astride the missile.

"Ready. Three. Two. One. Fire!"

Louie pushed a third button, and the missile smashed through the glass wall. Splinters and shards exploded in every direction.

Stephen crouched down so he wouldn't be cut by flying glass. He saw Louie sitting in one corner sucking a cut thumb.

Stephen had one glimpse of the missile silhouetted against the moon before he was aware that he was being suffocated by moths and butterflies fluttering against his nose. He woke up gasping, his chest heaving, and pushed them away from his face. A frog hopped off the bed, and a snake slithered after it.

Eight

*T*he craft fair was held in the village schoolyard, a large playing field with rickety bleachers at one end and a thick stand of trees at the other. Dew glittered on the grass. Wisps of night cloud drifted over the trees like forgotten dreams. The early morning sun shone through the thin air, a stunning white brilliance. The sun hurt Stephen's eyes. He shielded them with his hands and squinted at the fairground. A dozen or so trucks had been backed into a semi-circle. People were unloading boxes, setting up tables, fitting stalls together. There was little talk. It was too early for visiting: the cool mountain shadows invoked a powerful silence.

Uncle Adam parked the truck. Louie and Stephen unloaded the plywood panels. Two-by-fours had to be nailed into back supports for the framed panels. The sound of Uncle Adam's hammer echoed across the field. The boys lifted down two tables that came from the shop and set them end to end to serve as a counter. When the panels were in place, they helped Aunt Lise hang her weavings on the walls. Uncle Adam spread a woven cloth over the table and arranged his carvings on top. The fair was to begin with a ten o'clock parade along the village Main Street.

At nine-thirty the Old Timers' Kitchen Band assembled on the fairground for the parade. The air was a-jangle with toots, clashes and strums, all stirred together into a stew of discordant sound. Mrs Riley was among the musicians. Over her ample belly was a washtub, which she bonged with a wooden spoon. There was a woman playing a scrub board with a fork. Behind her a man whanged two pot covers like cymbals. Others were tooting on funnels and beating on pots and frying pans. All of them were smiling, relaxed, disarmed.

By ten o'clock the parade was lined up, ready to go. There was a clown at its head. He had a barrel chest and large flat feet. There was a red ball on his nose, pink patches on his cheeks and a ring of white around his mouth. He was wearing a curly orange wig. After the clown came the Old Timers' Kitchen Band. Following the band were the little kids: boys on small trikes festooned with crepe paper, girls wheeling doll carriages tied with bright ribbons. Behind them rode Sludge and Willard on their motorbikes. The motorbikes were decorated with crepe paper rosettes and ribbon.

"Wimps," Louie muttered. He glared at the bubble helmets in their floral disguise.

A Mountie marched past, his uniform red as an autumn maple leaf.

The small parade left the playing-field and marched down Main Street, past the general store, the hardware store, the bank, the lumber yard, the drug store and the church, where it turned around and marched back. People stood on the sidelines laughing and clapping. The clown grinned, showing large, square teeth. He poked little kids as he passed, patted them on their heads and handed out candies. Louie thought that if his sister Mad were here she'd be in the parade somewhere, probably riding her bike decorated with flowers. If Selena were here, Stephen thought, she'd want to be at the head of the parade. His sister liked attention.

When the parade returned to the fairgrounds, Louie and Stephen went to the Barrows' stall. Two people were already there talking to Uncle Adam about his carvings.

"There's no need for you boys to stay here," Aunt Lise said. "But come back in a while to spell us."

Stephen and Louie wandered around and looked at the stalls brimming with pottery, stained glass, crocheting, knitting, paintings, metal sculp-

ture, hooking, candles, quilts. It felt good knowing these beautiful things were here, but the boys
weren't much interested in them.

The fair soon became crowded. The clown was
still strolling around giving away balloons and
candies. Despite his comical face, he had a bold,
heavy way of moving that jogged something in
Stephen's mind, but he didn't know what it was.
The Mountie stood in the centre of the crowd having his picture taken; he looked strong and wise
and just.

They came to the recreational area of the fair.
This was where the schoolground slide, swings
and teeter-totters were. A log had been put into
the wading pool. Log-Rolling Contest at Four
O'clock, a cardboard sign read. Nearby, a large
barrel was filled with mysteriously wrapped packages. There was a fishing pole and a sign that said
Take Your Chance for a Dollar.

Stephen paid a dollar and won a maze, a plastic window with water droplets trapped inside
it.

They came to a horseshoe game: A Quarter a
Throw: Three Bull's-Eyes Win You a Prize. Louie
paid the quarters and made three bull's-eyes in a
row. He won a large teddy bear.

"I'll give it to Mad," he said.

Another stuffed animal for the zoo Mad kept
on her bed would help make up for the hole in
the boat.

They wandered around until they were hungry; then they headed for the food stalls.

The food stalls were at the opposite end of the field. Louie bought them each a hot dog, and Stephen bought two bottles of orange pop. They took these to the picnic tables behind the stalls, selecting a table away from the others. When they had sat down, they found themselves facing a display of trikes and bicycles decorated for the parade. A sign had been hung on a set of handlebars: Judging at Three O'clock.

Louie's eyes narrowed.

"Are we looking at the same thing?"

"Probably."

Behind the row of trikes and bicycles were two motorbikes.

"They look stupid with that junk on them," Stephen said. "Besides, this contest is for little kids."

"It wouldn't be fair if they won a prize," Louie said. "They don't deserve to win."

Sludge's motorbike was still festooned with crepe paper rosettes.

"I bet his grandmother made those flowers," Stephen said. That seemed to make it all the more unfair.

The boys set down their food and sauntered towards the motorbikes. Pretending to admire, they circled until the tables were empty of people.

"You keep an eye out," Louie said.

So while Stephen scanned the edges of the crowd, Louie ripped the rosettes off Sludge's motorbike and stuffed them into his pockets. Willard had woven crepe paper streamers around the spokes of his wheels. Louie crouched down and yanked these off too. Some of the decorations wouldn't come away, but he was satisfied that both motorbikes had been knocked out of the running. Compared to the other entries they wouldn't stand a chance. He managed to hide the decorations in a litter barrel before a family claimed a picnic table. He and Stephen gulped down their food. Louie picked up the teddy bear.

"We'd better go back," he said.

When they reached the stall, Stephen noticed that there were only a few carvings and weavings left. His aunt and uncle were smiling happily.

"We've been rushed off our feet," Aunt Lise said. "Most of our stuff has been sold already."

"And we need a break," Uncle Adam said. He showed Louie the money box and the receipt book.

The boys sat on chairs behind the counter and waited for customers. Most of the people who came were tourists asking questions the boys couldn't answer. A woman came by carrying a baby. While she fingered a set of book-ends, the baby spilled orange juice over a woven apron. The woman moved away without buying anything. Stephen wiped up the sticky mess with a paper bag. By now the sun was high overhead, beating down on them. The crowd milled past, laughing and eating. Once Stephen looked up and saw Sludge and Willard glaring at him. He looked away.

His aunt and uncle returned.

"Do you want to see the parade entries judged?" Aunt Lise said. "The judging's at three o'clock."

"Nah," Louie said quickly. "You go. We'd rather stay here." His parents gave him an odd look, but they went away.

At four o'clock they returned and insisted the boys go watch the log rolling.

"You've been stuck here for two hours," Aunt Lise said. "Now scoot."

So Stephen and Louie went to the wading pond to watch the log rollers. They were careful to stand on the edge of the crowd beside the Mountie.

Sludge and Willard stood across from them.

Stephen didn't pay much attention to the log rollers. He took the maze out of his pocket and began fiddling with it. Beneath its plastic window, drops of water pursued each other through a labyrinth of alleys and dead-ends. Stephen tilted the maze from side to side, trying to get the droplets to merge, but each remained separate, bent on its own course.

By the time the log-rolling contest was over, Sludge and Willard had worked their way closer. The Mountie had moved away. The crowd was thinning rapidly.

Sludge and Willard pursued them through the crowd.

In the middle of the field, a man dressed as a cowboy was organizing a square dance. People were being pushed back to clear a circular space. Stephen felt himself being shoved against Sludge. A fist slammed into his back. He ducked beneath a man's arm and elbowed his way through a knot of giggling girls. His back hurt where Sludge had belted him. He glanced around. There was no sign of Louie, but Sludge was ploughing through the girls, coming after him. Stephen pushed through the maze to the edge of the crowd. He ran up the field until he reached the stall. Louie was already there behind the counter. Quickly Stephen wedged himself in beside him.

Aunt Lise and Uncle Adam were talking to a heavyset man who was leaning across the counter. It was Mr Soper. Beside him stood a thin woman with hollow cheeks and dark eyes with greyish smudges beneath.

"I been wondering what you people were up to over there," Mr Soper was saying. "I said to Rose here, them Barrows must be well heeled to pull up stakes and move up here just like that. Most folks who live here was born here, can't afford to go noplace else. Isn't that what I said, Rose?"

Mrs Soper offered a nervous smile.

Stephen noticed that Mr Soper's cheeks were pink. Sunburn, he thought.

"I seen your stuff before it got sold. Your hobbies make pretty good money," Mr Soper said.

"They aren't hobbies," Uncle Adam said. "They're how we make our living."

"That a fact. Well, I can see why you'd want to get outta the city," Mr Soper went on conversationally. "Never took to it myself. Lived there once for a year, and that was a year too long. Never take my truck into one of them jungles if I don't have to. Too noisy. Too many people. Too much crime and violence. It gets on my nerves. I like peace and quiet. Don't I, Rose?"

Mrs Soper cast a nervous eye around the fairgrounds.

"It certainly is more peaceful here," Uncle Adam agreed.

Stephen and Louie squirmed uncomfortably.

Mr Soper took a toothpick out of his shirt pocket and began to pick his teeth.

"What did you do in the city," he said, "before you come here?"

Stephen noticed a faint ring of white around Mr Soper's mouth.

"I was a dentist," Uncle Adam said.

Mr Soper laughed. He had large, square teeth.

"That a fact. Well, now I'll know where to come if I get a toothache in the middle of the night."

Mrs Soper plucked her husband's arm.

"We'd better go, Mel," she said. "I'm awful tired."

Aunt Lise looked concerned.

"Are you feeling all right?" she said.

"The wife's ticker don't work too good," Mr

Soper said. "She's got to take it real easy. Eh, Rose?"

He put his arm around his wife and led her away.

It was then that Stephen saw the large flat feet. Mr Soper was still wearing them. Stephen couldn't help pointing.

"He was the clown!" he shouted. He felt tricked, cheated out of something important.

Willard and Sludge moved in behind the Sopers. The field was still being cleared for the dance.

People were taking down their stalls and packing them in their trucks. The Barrows dismantled theirs and loaded it onto the pickup along with the tables and chairs. Stephen and Louie climbed up and sat on the panels. Soon they were bumping homeward across the field. Mrs Riley had already packed up and gone back to her campground.

On their return, Stephen fiddled with the maze. No matter which way he tipped the plastic window, the water droplets refused to merge.

Louie sat back, the teddy bear between his knees, and watched dusk invade the mountains. Like mounted horsemen the shadows rode up the valley, their blue capes fanned out behind them. As the horsemen rode closer, Louie saw that they were carrying spears. The tips of the spears looked like faint stars glinting through azure dusk.

Nine

That night the boys went to sleep listening to strumming guitars and campfire songs. Human voices mingled with coyotes' yodelling in the starry night.

In the morning they were awakened by a transistor radio.

Louie stirred drowsily.

"Saturday," he murmured. He didn't need a calendar to tell him the weekend had arrived.

When they came into the kitchen, Uncle Adam was already up lighting a fire in the stove. He was wearing his bathing suit.

"How about a swim before breakfast?" he said.

Yesterday's sales had put him in a jovial mood. "Afterwards I'll womp up pancakes."

The boys fetched the towels, and the three of

them walked down the hill to the dock. The edges of the cove were still in shadow, but the centre gleamed like liquid emeralds. There was a gentle breeze. They climbed into *The Explorer*, and Louie rowed them out to the raft, where they sat, legs in the water, looking at the whiteness of their skin. The water made their flesh seem tender and unprotected. Behind them at Riley's they heard early morning stirrings as campers prepared their breakfasts. Three little kids splashed in the water off Riley's dock, outraging the mother duck. The duck quacked loudly, ordering her children out of the bulrushes nearby. The ducklings, paddling after their mother like furry cabooses, streamed away, heading for quieter water. A female hummingbird hovered over Stephen's red towel, mistaking it for a flower, until a male hummingbird swooped down to claim the towel as his territory.

Uncle Adam was first into the water, knifing the cool green with a light splash. Louie and Stephen jumped in, and the three of them stroked towards the cove mouth. Stephen liked swimming in this direction best. There was something exhilarating about moving towards a mountain so massive its white shoulders seemed to be holding up the sky. Stephen didn't think he had ever seen anything as beautiful as this snowy peak, luminous in the morning sun. In the early light, even the cave entrance looked benign, as harmless as a sleeping eye.

They flipped onto their backs and kicked lazily

back. The three little kids, oblivious to the sign spelling PRIVATE on the side of the raft, had paddled out in their dinghy and were jumping into the water. Uncle Adam didn't seem to mind their being on the raft, but it bothered Louie and Stephen. They were torn between maintaining ownership and deciding it didn't matter enough to spoil their swim.

Uncle Adam made the decision.

"Time for breakfast," he said and got into *The Explorer*.

When they reached their dock, Louie said, "Tonight we're camping out on the other side of the lake."

"Where it's quieter," Stephen pointed out.

Uncle Adam offered no resistance.

Back in the house they found Aunt Lise bundled up in her bathrobe drinking coffee at the kitchen table.

"I'm taking it easy today," she announced.

Louie told her about the campout.

"Keep an eye out for the weather. If it turns nasty, come back," she said. "And remember to keep your fire close to the lake."

As mountain people, the Barrows had become wary of fire. Two years before, a forest fire had wiped out an area of woods near the village dump. *The burn* people called it now: it was the place to go for fence poles. The trees stood up from the blackened soil like sharpened spears.

"They can use the fire ring Louie and I made,"

Adam said. Last summer he and Louie had camped on the other side of the lake. "It's safe enough."

Adam mixed up batter and began cooking pancakes. He removed the stove lid and held the cast iron frying pan directly over the coals because that arrangement was better for flipping. He flipped a pancake three feet in the air and caught it neatly.

"Wow," Stephen said.

"My record's five feet," his uncle boasted. He flipped the next one higher and missed. The pancake went into the fire.

Everyone laughed.

After breakfast Louie packed enough supplies to last three days. He didn't intend to come back before the campground was empty. Stephen checked his knapsack: rope, flashlight, matches, insect repellent, water canteen, suntan lotion — all there. He shoved in clothes and towels. Louie got out the pup tent, air mattresses and sleeping bags. It took several trips down the hill to *The Explorer* before they were ready.

"I'll ring the cowbell if we want you to come back," Aunt Lise said on their last trip down.

The lake was noisier than before. There were more strangers on their raft, adults now. From across the water came the sound of motorboats riling the lake surface with choppy waves.

Louie noticed the bald patch on *The Explorer*. It irked him that they still hadn't painted it.

"Just a minute," Stephen said. He monkeyed

up the ladder to the tree-lab and came back with their weapons. He stowed them beneath the camping gear. Then they were off.

They rowed over a shallow stretch of water to the cove mouth. Stephen, scanning the lake for trout, saw on the lake bottom the rusty barrel he and Louie had salvaged.

"Look what they've been up to now," he said. "Dumped the barrel back in."

Louie was silent. After what Sludge and Willard had done to his tree-lab, nothing surprised him.

He stopped at the beaver lodge to rest from rowing.

Stephen looked into the weeds beneath the boat, where moss covered beaver lodges like ancient underwater ruins.

"Have you ever seen the beaver?" he said. He was beginning to think it didn't exist.

"I saw him sunning himself on a log last summer," Louie said. "But that's all."

He rowed on.

The end of the lake was quieter. From here the sounds of swimmers were nothing more than faint echoes. They hauled the boat into the eel grass beside Angus's green canoe. A turtle, dozing on a fallen tree, slipped into the water. A great blue heron flapped up from the eel grass, dragging his feet across the tops of the sentinel firs.

"Must have a nest nearby," Louie said.

The fire ring was on the exposed flank of the

tree battalion. It occupied a flat space just wide enough for a small tent. Stephen would have preferred to camp on the inner side of the trees, but there they would be unable to light a fire.

They carried their equipment to the site and put up the pup tent. Then they blew up the air mattresses, readied their beds and set out utensils. By noon they were done. They made a lunch of bread and cheese. Louie opened two cans of apple juice. When the cans were empty he put them in a green garbage bag and tied it from a limb high in a fir tree. He did the same thing with their provisions, making sure they were out of reach of any bear who considered this his domain.

The sun was high overhead. The breeze had grown to a small wind, but it was pleasant and cooling. Stephen checked his knapsack, Louie picked up the water canteen and they started off.

The mountain towered above them, a mighty fortress. From here they could not see the cave mouth, because it was obscured by trees. The tip of the burnt tree stuck up like a flagless pole. They ducked beneath the sentinel firs, waded through the clearing of willows and began to climb the rugged slope towards the plateau. It was hot work, but the breeze helped. At the top of the plateau they flopped down wearily. Louie offered the water canteen. They were sitting at the edge of the forest of masks. Both of them were aware of the masks, bright as wet stones, hanging from the trees behind them, but they were careful not to look that way. They knew the masks would draw them in the way the lake drew in their reflections, and they did not want to be drawn in. They especially did not want to be drawn into the clearing where Angus worked. He wouldn't approve of their going up to the cave.

Beyond the plateau the woods grew thickly. The boys had to break trail, pushing past heavy branches and thick underbrush. Their faces became scratched from sharp branches, their hair matted with twigs. Stephen's cheek was slapped red when a branch snapped back suddenly. They made slow, noisy progress.

"The animals will hear us a mile away," Louie said.

On the other side of this barrier they came to an alpine meadow carpeted with flowers. Louie thought of picking flowers for his mother's lampshades, but he didn't want to take the time. Going through the meadow was easy. Grass swished silkily as they passed. The meadows sloped upward to an escarpment with a rock pile at its base.

Stephen heard a high, shrill whistle. He jumped nervously: he had never been this far into a wilderness before.

But Louie had been this far with his father.

"It's only a marmot," he laughed.

Stephen looked up and saw a blob of greyish-tan fur on top of the rock pile. It scuttled into a crevice. There was a skittering of small rocks.

The meadow gave way to a precipice. Stephen looked down on more trees, a forest that stretched on endlessly. Towering above it was the black compass tree.

The woods they now entered were sparser. It was a forest of jack pine. There were brown pellets: animal droppings roughly spaced in a line they could follow.

"An elk path," Louie said. "On their way to a hidden valley."

"Why is it hidden?"

"No one knows for sure where they go in the summer," Louie explained.

These woods continued for a long way. Stephen noticed that the sun was dropping lower and lower; it was now a flaming ball balanced on the tree-tops. The afternoon was rapidly slipping away. He had noticed that it got dark earlier in the mountains. In the city, pavement and skyscrapers bounced back the sunlight long into summer evenings, but here the deep valleys drew the shadows around them like enfolding cloaks.

Eventually they came to a ridge of high rocks. The rocks were so large there were crevasses between. The ridge zigzagged up the mountainside like the Great Wall of China. The boys scrambled on top of the wall and looked down. Below them the mountain swept away to a deep chasm at the bottom of which was a narrow thread of green water. Ahead was another mountain range.

The only way open to them was to follow the rock wall upward.

They began their ascent by climbing over rocks on the inner edge of the wall. This was tiring work but the quickest route, since the bushes grew jungle thick against the rocks. A breeze kept them cool. They climbed until they were within sight of the cave.

Stephen looked up. As Louie had said, the cave was larger than it looked from below. It was a huge, eye-shaped hole with an overhanging cliff that rose steeply in a craggy forehead. The eye hole was completely blank, yet Stephen felt it glaring at him. He shivered. The hair on his forearms came up in stiff prickles. Could the Wild Man of the Woods see them?

After a while Louie said, ''It shouldn't be too hard to get to.''

''Let's go,'' Stephen said. He started forward. Something was pulling him up to the cave.

''No,'' Louie said sharply. ''It's too late. If we go up now we may have to come back in the dark. Now that we know the way, we'll come back early tomorrow.''

''Aw, c'mon,'' Stephen said.

''Go if you want,'' Louie said. ''I'm going back.''

Stephen started climbing. After a while he turned around. Louie had disappeared into the bushes. Stephen stopped. What if he got lost up here? But there was the compass tree, wasn't there? He looked at the tree. For an instant he imagined he saw a huge, bulging head skewered on top of the pole, a face with ugly teeth and fierce eyes that grinned evilly at him. Stephen shook his head and the face disappeared. But it left him scared and shaken.

"Louie!" he yelled and stumbled down the mountain. "Wait for me!"

Louie hadn't gone far. He was sitting in the bushes eating. He handed the plastic bag to Stephen.

"Have some gorp," he said.

Stephen took a handful. He tried to get mostly Smarties but ended up with cornflakes and raisins. He popped them into his mouth. The sound of his own munching and swallowing steadied him. He was relieved to be in the bushes, out of sight of the cave and the black pole.

"We should ask Angus about that tree," he said. He wondered if there was a connection between it and the mask. "It looks like it's been there a long time."

"Like the Wild Man of the Woods," Louie said.

There was a rumbling sound from inside the cave. The sky darkened.

"Let's get out of here," Louie said.

They went back through the jack pine, recrossed the alpine meadow and picked up their broken trail through the thick forest. As Louie had predicted, it was faster going down. They came to the plateau. The wind was much fuller now. Cool air flowed across their skins like water.

This time they allowed the forest of masks to draw them in. The clearing was cool and smelled of clean cedar. The masks swung on the ends of their ropes. They passed Coyote and Bear and the mask with the divided face. Stephen felt that he was being watched, but kindly. The wind lifted the back of his shirt. It felt soothing against his sunburn.

"I wonder if Angus has finished the wind mask," he said.

They went on until they came to the tree where Angus had been working. The mask was gone. Nothing remained but a large naked square where it had been cut out of the massive trunk.

"I hope it didn't hurt the tree," Stephen said. He rubbed his hand over the hole.

Angus wasn't in the clearing either, but the wind mask was on the work-bench. It had been freshly painted. Its face was dark blue, its eyes and mouth chalk white. Stephen held his hand in front of the face. He felt a wind coming through the mouth hole.

It was the same wind scudding the clouds overhead, darkening the woods, rocking the trees. The rocking trees made Stephen feel protected. His eyes searched the trees for the mask carver, but there was no sign of him.

"He's not here," he said.

Louie noticed that the teepee flap was closed.

"Maybe he's asleep," he said.

Stephen was surprised by the thought of Angus sleeping. The giant was so different from anyone he knew that he had come to think of him as someone who was more than human, someone who didn't need to sleep or eat.

"C'mon. Let's go. I'm getting hungry," Louie said.

They were re-entering the woods when a deep voice called them back.

"What do you want?" It was coming from inside the teepee.

"Nothing," Stephen shouted back. "We just wanted to ask you something."

"What?" the voice boomed out like a drum.

"We wanted to ask about that big black tree," Stephen shouted. He felt silly having a conversation with someone he couldn't see.

The tent flap opened and Angus emerged yawning. White hair cascaded down his shoulders like a hanging waterfall. "Well, now that you've got me awake I might as well get up," he grumbled, but he didn't sound very cross. He sat down on the stump stool and began braiding his pigtail.

"That big black tree is the fire tree," he said. "It's the oldest tree in the valley. There's a story about it that goes back to the days when Coyote tried to kill the sun."

"Kill the sun," Louie protested. "No one can kill the sun."

Stephen watched Angus braid a leather thong into his hair.

"People know that now, but they didn't know it then," he said.

"Yeah," Louie said. "They didn't know about light-years, red shifts and black holes."

"But they still wanted to know why things were," Angus said. He tied his braid with a thong.

"What did they want to know about the sun?"

"Who can say?" the old man said. "Maybe they wanted to know why it was always there burning hot and bright, giving us heat and light. One thing is sure, it had to do with power."

"So what's the story?" Stephen said.

"Well, the story is about Coyote who wanted Big Sun's power, so he shot arrows up into the sky trying to kill it. But his plan backfired. One of the arrows caught fire. It fell back to earth and started a forest fire. All of the trees burned except the one you saw. Coyote climbed it and was safe, though the tree blackened to what it is now. My people say that when Coyote points his nose like an arrow into the night sky, he's remembering his defeat."

Stephen remembered the ugly mask he had seen on top of the tree.

"Is that what happened to the Wild Man of the Woods?" he said. "Was it defeated too?"

Angus leaped up; his black eyes sparked

angrily. "Why do you keep asking about that evil mask?" he rumbled.

Stephen and Louie backed up from those eyes, flashing like lightning. Their answer was silence. The silence grew. Around them the trees groaned in the breeze, their branches swaying like dancers' scarves.

Angus sat down, his shoulders slumped, the flame in his eyes dwindled.

"The Wild Man of the Woods was never defeated," he said heavily. "It was only hidden, out of harm's way."

"Why wasn't it defeated?" Stephen said.

"People were afraid. The mask destroyed too many of us."

"It was a cannibal mask," Stephen said. "I read it in a book."

"Books!" Angus said scornfully. "What do they know? The truth is in the masks."

There it was again.

"But is it true it was a cannibal mask?" Stephen persisted.

"For some it was," Angus said. "When their worst enemy was hunger."

Stephen imagined a black mouth, white flesh, red blood.

Louie didn't like the turn in the conversation. "We'd better go, Steve," he said uncomfortably. He was also worried about the weather. If it turned nasty, they'd have to go home. "There's a wind blowing up."

Angus smiled. "It's the mask," he said. He reached out a big hand and turned the wind mask so that it faced east-west instead of north-south. "Now you will see a change."

The change did not come immediately.

But afterwards, as Stephen and Louie were walking through the forest of masks, they noticed that the heads were no longer swinging to and fro but rocking gently like the trees.

Ten

Dusk was falling when Louie and Stephen reached their campsite. The first thing they did was light a fire. Louie crumpled up newspapers he had brought along while Stephen broke off dead branches from the lower trunks of the sentinel firs. Then he scrounged around the forest floor until he had gathered a large supply of firewood. Louie opened two cans of spaghetti and set them in a pan of hot water. He cut slabs of cheese and laid them on top of the spaghetti. When the cheese was melted he removed the cans from the pan, handling them gingerly because they were hot. They ate their spaghetti with chunks of bread and tins of grape juice. Stephen was impressed by the fact that there were no dishes to clean afterwards, only two spoons, which Louie swished in the hot-water pan. After the food and the garbage had been rehoisted up the tree, they sat around the fire toasting marshmallows saved from their food cache.

By now it had become dark. On the black water, their fire gleamed like torchlight. Stars came winking on. Stephen picked out Big Bear and Orion's Belt. It was reassuring to be able to do this, to know that night after night the stars were there in their right places. It wasn't the same with space ships, UFOs or satellites, which came and went and could not be relied on always to be where you wanted them. This was why he liked the stars better than the moon. He didn't like the fact that there were times in the month when you couldn't see the moon. Of course that was because the moon existed in darkness and relied on the sun for light. Coyote hadn't bothered shooting arrows at the moon.

Stephen looked at the moon; it wasn't as round as it had been the night he arrived. Part of the circle was already blurred. In another week it would disappear altogether. Stephen noticed that the moon in the water was brighter than the moon in the sky. He stared at the water moon. It looked like a silver keyhole in the door of the lake.

The moon reminded Louie of his sister Mad. He and Mad often went swimming at night.

"Let's go skinny-dipping," he said. His fingers were sticky with marshmallow.

They piled more wood on the fire, hung their

clothes and towels on a nearby branch to warm while they were swimming, and slipped into the lake. The water flowed around their naked bodies like dark silk, cool and caressing. The boys floated on their backs, keeping close together. Stephen was aware of the deep water below. He remembered the large footprints he had seen on the shallow cove bottom. He thought of lake monsters, serpents and prehistoric reptiles who moved so slowly they had lost the race with time. He tried to manoeuvre himself onto the moon's silvery path. He thought if he could reach it the water there would be lighter and safer. And if he could go still farther and reach the silver keyhole, what then? If he held his breath and dived through that hole, would he enter some place he'd never been, a place on the other side of the world, a place where there were columns of pale stone, people in long white robes? He thought of his father in Greece. His father would be on a boat now in a sea somewhere between the islands of the Aegean Sea. Stephen wondered if the moon made a keyhole in the water there too. He stroked hard towards the silvery path.

"Hey, where are you going?" Stephen heard Louie's voice in his ear. "We'd better get back. It's better not to swim too far from shore at night."

Stephen lifted his face out of the lake. Water glittered on his lashes like moon gems. He saw a fire flickering on a far shore. They had come a surprising distance, but he was still no closer to the keyhole.

They swam back without stopping and hauled themselves out of the water, shivering in the night air. They towelled themselves dry and put on their warmed clothes. Then they hunched over the fire. The smoke helped keep the mosquitoes away. A loon called from the reeds to its mate. It was a melodious, melancholy sound, a celebration of sadness. But the loon didn't make Stephen feel sad. He felt clean and good.

From across the lake came the sounds of camp-ground parties, but the sounds were muted, soft. The light from their log house on the hill quivered like a candle's flame. Stephen stared contentedly at the stars.

There was a loud splash nearby. His head jerked down.

"What was that?" he said.

Blinded by the firelight, Louie peered into the dark.

"Must be the beaver."

There was another splash, lighter this time. Then another.

"You sure it's the beaver?"

"No. It could be a trout. Sometimes they rise at night. The small ones make splashes like that."

There was a louder splash as something flat hit the water.

"A beaver's tail?" Stephen said.

There was a sharp click.

Then came the first shot — a loud bang.

"Down!" Louie screamed.

Stephen ducked. There was another shot.

"Make for the trees!" Louie yelled. Flat on their bellies they wormed their way across the ground, beneath the sentinel firs, until they reached the thick willows. Their hearts thumped loudly between their ears, which were scratched and bleeding from sharp branches. Mosquitoes whined above their heads. They heard one more shot.

"Those jerks!" Louie fumed. "Wait until I get my hands on them. I'll choke them. I'll kick their faces in. I'll . . ."

"You'd better stop that," they heard a frightened voice say. It was Sludge. "You want to get us in trouble?"

"I'm only trying to give them a good scare," Willard whined. "Besides they're not real bullets. They're blanks."

There was the splutter of an engine.

"That's to teach you guys a lesson!" Willard yelled into the trees. "Keep away from our motorbikes and we'll leave you alone. OK, Sludge, rev 'er up."

"First I got to get the paddle I dropped in the water," Sludge said.

"You can't see it in the dark, Stupid," Willard said. "We'll get it tomorrow."

"We'd better," Sludge bleated, "or I'll be in trouble."

The motor coughed, took hold, then roared away.

For a while after they had gone, Stephen lay where he was. He was shaking so hard he could feel the leaves around him tremble.

Louie stood up. ''They didn't come close to hurting us,'' he scoffed, but there was a catch in his voice. ''C'mon.''

They sat around the fire again, but the night's magic had gone. Stephen sat as close to the flame as he could without getting burned, but still he couldn't get warm. He felt a cold wind on the back of his neck. Never had the stars seemed so far away.

''Let's hit the sack,'' Louie said. He doused the flames, and they crawled into their sleeping bags.

Sleep did not come easily. The night was silent. Even the campground across the lake was smothered by darkness. Once Louie thought he heard someone outside. He got up and looked through the tent flap, but he saw no one. The wind fanned the moonlit walls of the pup tent, moving them in and out like bellows. The breathing tent soothed Louie, and eventually he slipped into a deep and dreamless sleep.

But for Stephen sleep brought another violent nightmare.

He was standing in an open field. Opposite him were two figures. He couldn't see their faces because they had black hoods masking them. They looked like dummies, the kind used for target practice.

He knew from the feel of dry cotton against his wet mouth that he was wearing a hood too. The hood made his head feel disembodied, separate from the rest of him as if it were swinging all by itself from a tree or was stuck up on a pole. The strange thing was that, though his body was disconnected from his head, he could feel something heavy on his shoulder. It was as if he were carrying an enormous load, a weight that made him tired, so very tired.

He looked at the hooded figures. This time he saw the guns at their sides. The figures were lifting the guns to their shoulders, preparing to fire at someone. In one panic-stricken moment he realized they were the firing squad. They weren't dummies, he was. He heard a sharp click, then another. Fear tore at his stomach.

With tremendous effort he lifted his hand to the weight on his shoulder. He knew now that it was a heavy gun that had been weighing him down. Slowly, inch by painful inch, he crooked his index finger around the trigger. He had to shoot them before they shot him. But he couldn't move his finger. He couldn't press hard enough. His finger was paralysed. It was too late, too late. He threw down the gun. He couldn't defend himself. He pulled off his hood and screamed. And as he screamed he saw the ugly mask on top of a blackened tree go up in flames.

"Wake up, Steve," Louie reached over and shook his cousin. "Wake up!"

Stephen opened his eyes and stared at him.

"They were going to shoot me," he mumbled.

"It was a nightmare," Louie said.

"They tried to kill us," Stephen said.

"No they didn't," Louie said. "They were shooting blanks to save us, the jerks." His eyes narrowed. "We'll have to show them. This time we'll really have to show them. It's what they need."

"They're going to need a lot," Stephen said.

Louie stuck his head through the tent opening. The sun was up but partially hidden by cloud. The wind riffled the lake a sandpaper grey. The campground was silent. The air was empty of birdsong.

"It's still early," he said. "Let's go back to sleep." He crawled into his sleeping bag and closed his eyes.

But he couldn't sleep. His body wanted to, but his mind was wide awake. He couldn't stop thinking about last night. The knowledge that Willard and Sludge had been hiding in the reeds all that time spying on them while they were making their fire, eating supper, roasting marshmallows, skinny-dipping, upset him. That their most private actions and their pale nakedness should be known to those geeks angered him more than being shot at. Of course Sludge and Willard had gone too far with that gun. Shooting at someone whether or not you meant to hurt them was a serious offence. They should go down to the village and tell the Mountie about it, that's what they should do. That would end this fight. Or would it? The Mountie would come up and talk to Sludge's grandmother and Willard's parents. Louie took some satisfaction in imagining this, in seeing Willard and Sludge backed into a corner, trembling like a pair of terrified rabbits in front of the law. Willard would probably get in trouble with his father, and Sludge wouldn't be able to ride that stupid motorbike for a while. Of course Sludge and Willard would tell on them. They'd tell about their tires, about the decorations being ripped off their precious machines, even though they wouldn't have won the prize anyway. They'd tell about the dummy being strung up on Soper's clothesline. Mr Soper would come over and complain about their being like all those city folks he didn't have much use for. Mrs Riley wouldn't be so friendly with his parents anymore, and his parents needed friends around here. The more Louie thought about it the more he decided telling the Mountie wouldn't work. It wouldn't really end the fight. It might even make it worse. What would have to happen was for him and Steve to give Sludge and Willard a big enough scare that they'd call it quits and leave them alone, once and for all.

Stephen couldn't get back to sleep either. He was afraid to. He was afraid that if he closed his eyes the nightmare would return. He was tired of these stupid nightmares. The cruel pictures drained him, made him feel half dead. He wanted to stop them. The way to do this, he decided, was to fight back harder, to beat those bullies at their own game. Now that he had come this far he wasn't going to back off. If you didn't stand up to bullies you'd be running away from them for the rest of your life. Besides, he and Louie couldn't quit while Sludge and Willard were ahead. Those jerks had thrown mud at them, messed up their towels, bugged them with their motorbikes, cut the raft wires, put a hole in Mad's boat, smashed Louie's tree-lab, dumped the barrel back into the lake and shot at them. So what if Louie's knife had slipped going into Willard's tire? That had been mostly an accident. So what if they'd strung up a dummy and ripped those stupid ribbons off their motorbikes? That was nothing compared with what Sludge and Willard had done. The score wasn't even close. *Keep away from our motorbikes and we'll leave you alone.* Willard would taunt them with that because he and Sludge were so far ahead. Stephen knew the war was getting dangerous, but that only meant that this time he and Louie would have to do a more thorough job of getting even.

Stephen watched the orange walls of the pup tent breathe in and out with his chest, lifting and falling, lifting and falling. The wind was rising again. Had Angus turned the mask back to north-south? Was he walking around in the woods with the mask on, turning his head in one direction and then the other, churning up the weather? Did he really have that kind of power? And if he did, was the power in the mask or in Angus? Stephen looked across the tent at Louie.

"I've been thinking," he said. "If we could give Willard and Sludge a big scare with that mask, it would fix them all right."

"Yeah," Louie said. "It sure would."

"It's risky, though. All that evil stuff Angus was warning us about," Stephen said.

"Never mind that," Louie said briskly. "Like Mrs Riley said, it's probably gobbledygook."

"But what if it's true?" Stephen said.

"Willard and Sludge took a risk coming over here with that gun."

Louie got up and looked out of the tent.

"Weather's kind of fuzzy. We'd better hurry if we want to get up to that cave before it storms."

They got into their clothes and went outside. Louie lit a small fire. Stephen fetched water from the lake. The surface was so rough he couldn't see the reflection of his face. When he had scooped up a potful of water and was walking back with it, he saw two large footprints beside their tent. The front part of the feet was indistinct, but the shape of the heels was clear enough. Some of the water sloshed out of the pot onto the prints.

"Louie," he said. "Look. Footprints."

"There you go again," Louie said.

He poked the fire.

"Those heels. They're huge."

"Look, we could've made those marks ourselves. We stood right there with wet feet when
we came out of the lake, remember?"

He took the pot and put it on the fire.

But Stephen couldn't shake loose the picture
of a Sasquatch or Wendigo prowling this territory.
Or maybe it was Angus. Stephen almost preferred
to think it was a Sasquatch. Now that they were
going up to the cave he didn't like the thought of
the old man's snooping around their tent last
night.

"Better get the food down," Louie said.

Stephen untied the rope, lowered the green
plastic bag and took out provisions.

After they had gulped down two packages of
instant oatmeal, they ate half-burnt toast smeared
with peanut butter. Louie took out more gorp,
and they rehoisted their food cache, washed their
bowls and spoons and packed Stephen's
knapsack.

"Better take extra rope," Louie said, "We may
need it."

Stephen went to *The Explorer* for the rope. He
saw their weapons stowed on the bottom of the
dory. He brought them back and handed Louie
his spear. Then he stuck his sword through a belt
loop so his hands would be free to carry the
shield. He shrugged on his knapsack.

Louie doused the fire.

"We're off," he said.

Their climb up the mountain was slow at first.

They avoided the forest of masks. Even so, they felt they were being watched. As they went deeper into the wilderness this feeling left them. They became determined and fierce, their faces hardened into sullen masks. They crossed the alpine meadow, waded through the pine woods and came to the fire tree. It towered over the wilderness like a warning, its sharp point arrowing into low clouds. By now the sky had become thickly packed with dirty lamb's-wool clouds. Ahead of them was the sound of low rumbling. When they broke out of the trees and came to the rock wall, there was a blink of lightning. They looked up at the cave. For an instant it seemed that the light was coming from inside the cave like the glint of an angry eye. They followed the zigzag wall until they were directly across from the cave.

Louie looked at the narrow path cut into the grey flank of mountain. It was a sheer drop to the bottom of the talus slope, where a thread of grey water needled through the valley floor. They had to cross the path to get to the cave. Fortunately the path was short and there was enough rope. Louie took the rope out of Stephen's knapsack and cut it in half. He tied one length around his waist and then looped it around a twisted jack pine that grew over the cliff's edge. Though badly deformed, the tree was sturdy enough to hold his weight.

"If we lose our footing, at least we won't go to the bottom," he said. "I'll cross first."

Using his spear for balance, Louie braced himself and walked across the thin path like an acrobat walking a tightrope. He didn't dare look down. One glance into the valley and he was sure to lose his footing. He walked steadily, swiftly, and came to the cave mouth. Once he was on firm footing he untied the rope from his waist and coiled it around a large stone on the cave floor. Then he turned to help Stephen.

Stephen shrugged off his knapsack; he thought it might slip from one side to another and knock him off balance. Instead he took the sword out of his belt loop; holding it in one hand, he grasped the shield in the other to keep himself steady. Like Louie he dared not look down, but kept his eyes on his feet and the narrow path in front of him. He saw Louie's face come into view. He saw an outstretched hand. He grabbed the hand and it pulled him into the cave.

Eleven

"We did it," Stephen said. He untied the rope from his waist and coiled it around the same rock Louie had used.

Despite their success in getting across the slope, neither one felt light-hearted. Because of the over-hanging forehead the cave was dark, the air heavy and thick. The weight of dead air pressed against Stephen's chest. He coughed.

"I can't see a thing in here," he said. He was annoyed at himself for leaving the knapsack containing the flashlight on the other side.

"You got any matches?" he said.

Louie dug a match out of his pocket and struck it against a rock. Immediately the flame flared up, and he saw pictures on the wall.

"Look at these," he said. His voice bounced

off the walls of the cave and came back to him, making him feel insignificant.

The pictures were faint. There were smudges of red faded like blood stains and dark lines deeply incised into the rock. By following the lines the boys deciphered the shapes of strange creatures, half-man, half-beast, dressed in skins. One had the antlered head of a stag, another the head of a bear. Both had sharp claws for hands. Still another had a human face but a coyote's ears.

"The first masks," Steven murmured, and the match went out.

"They look like medicine men to me," Louie spoke into the dark. He shivered and lit another match.

It was true. The creatures were holding bone rattles and furred sticks.

"They must go back to the Ice Age," Louie said. He followed the pictures on the rough wall. He felt better having something to hold onto, a thread that wove back through time. Louie's foot hit a hollow rounded object. He lit another match and looked down.

A human skull leered up at him. He dropped the match. In its wavering light he caught a glimpse of other bones spread across the cave floor. The match went out.

"I have only one match left," he said.

Stephen's foot kicked another skull, smaller than the first. It clattered down a slight incline towards the back of the cave.

"I wonder if the Wild Man of the Woods is here," he whispered.

Lightning flashed in the mouth of the cave. In its blinding light Stephen saw a greenish-black mask on a rock shelf in front of him. Above a hooked nose that crooked under itself, two eyes caught fire. They glowed redly. Stephen felt two eye holes drill into his chest. He fell forward onto his knees and looked up at the mask. There was a rumble of thunder. Two rows of shark's teeth grated against each other. Stephen felt as if his bones were being ground into a fine powder. There was a clacking noise cold as icicles.

Stephen saw a hand touch the tangled hair. But before Louie could pick up the mask, Stephen reached up, grabbed the face and slipped it over his. Then he stood up.

"I am the Wild Man of the Woods," he bellowed.

Lightning flashed; for an instant the cave was filled with sulphurous light.

"That'll give Willard and Sludge a big scare," Louie said admiringly, but his voice shook.

The inside of the mask smelled musty. There was a layer of something powdery lining it that clung to Stephen's skin. "I am the Wendigo," he roared.

Thunder rumbled.

Stephen staggered forward under the weight of the mask.

Instinctively Louie backed up towards the cave entrance. He tripped over a skull.

"C'mon, Steve," he said. "Take that thing off. We only want to use it for Willard and Sludge."

But Stephen had no intention of taking it off. He liked wearing the mask. It gave him a feeling of immense power. He felt he could beat up anyone who crossed his path. He could knock the heads off not only Willard, Sludge and Terry Mulcaster but anyone who'd ever bullied him.

"You know Angus told us it was dangerous," Louie said. His voice was trembling. "Take off that mask!"

"What mask?" the voice rumbled. Stephen was beginning to feel that the Wild Man of the Woods was not a mask, that it had become his head, that *he* was the Wild Man of the Woods. His head no longer felt too heavy for the rest of his body.

"Take it off!" Louie reached for the mask.

Wild Man pushed the hand roughly aside.

"You heard me!" Louie's voice quavered.

Wild Man gave him a shove. This boy was beginning to make him angry. Wild Man drilled him with his red eyes.

Red is the fire, the fight, the fight, he chanted.

Louie groped for his spear and whacked it against the mask, trying to knock it off. But Wild Man deflected the blow with his sword. He knocked Louie to the cave floor, grabbed the end of the rope and tied it around Louie's wrists and ankles. Then he ground his teeth together with satisfaction. This boy was being a pest, yammering at him to take off a mask. But he had fixed him. Wild Man wanted no one to get in his way. He would break out of this cave. He would avenge the bullies of this world and no one, least of all this puny-fleshed boy, was going to stop him.

"Aw c'mon, Steve," Louie said. "You're carrying this too far."

Shut your face, Wild Man growled. Already he had forgotten Louie's name. He picked up the sword and shield and left the cave. He did not bother using the rope but crossed the narrow path in superhuman strides. As he went he chanted,

> *Break away the night, the night*
> *Tear away the flesh*
> *Red is the fire, the fight, the fight*
> *My thirst for blood is black.*

From inside the cave Louie heard the voice mumbling its horrible chant. It didn't sound like Steve. In fact the person inside the mask didn't seem to *be* Steve: it was someone else. Steve wasn't the sort of person to knock down a friend and tie him up for no reason. It was as if he'd gone wild, completely out of control. Louie heard rocks sliding; he held his breath. Steve had used the rope to tie him up instead of to help get himself safely across the slope. What if his cousin fell down the mountainside? He wouldn't stop until he reached the bottom where the stream ran. By then he'd be dead. But Steve didn't fall. Louie heard him on the other side of the slope slamming his sword against a tree, chanting those strange words. Louie slowly let out his breath. Now that his cousin had made it across he had better see to his own safety. He had to get out of this creepy cave.

Fortunately the rope had been carelessly knotted. He wriggled his hands out of their loops without too much trouble. Then he untied his ankles. Holding onto the rope and carrying his spear, he got himself across the slope. He untied the rope from the gnarled tree and stuffed them inside the knapsack; then he glanced at the sky. The clouds were ominously low. Behind them he heard the rumble of thunder. A drop of rain splattered his cheek. He'd have to find Steve. See if he couldn't knock that terrifying mask off his head before he got himself in trouble.

Instead of following the rock wall, his cousin had gone through the bushes, leaving a trail of broken bushes in his wake. Louie followed this crooked trail at a safe distance. He wanted the advantage of seeing Steve before Steve saw him. The trail continued until the fire tree. Crouched behind a protective screen of leaves, Louie watched his cousin. Steve was hacking at the charred pole with a jack-knife. It was *his* jack-knife, Louie thought, the one Steve had given him as a present. He must have taken it from the knapsack. What a strange thing to be doing with it. Steve had completely flipped his lid, gone wacko.

As Steve gouged and hacked at the tree, Louie heard him chant,

> *Break away the night, the night*
> *Tear away the flesh*
> *Red is the fire, the fight, the fight*
> *My thirst for blood is black.*

The evil head wobbled from side to side, keeping an unsteady rhythm.

Hearing this dreadful chant made Louie angry with himself and with Steve. Why had they been so foolish to think they could use an evil mask to get even with Willard and Sludge? In fact, getting even no longer seemed important. The more he watched the mask wobble from side to side, the more convinced Louie became that he'd better not try to knock it off; at least, he had better not try it alone. Steve was armed with a sword and a jack-knife. If Louie failed to get the mask off, his cousin might turn on him again. Steve seemed a lot bigger now that he was the Wild Man of the Woods. He might tie Louie to the black tree, tighter this time, and go off and leave him here. Then Louie'd be unable to get help.

Abruptly the Wild Man of the Woods broke off his chant so he could hear Louie's thoughts. His head swivelled around so that the two red eyes burned through the leaves. Louie ducked down and willed himself into stone so that shaking leaves wouldn't give him away. Terror tripled the seconds racing with the loudness of his heart. The red eyes drilled through the leaves around Louie.

Louie smelled something burning. After what seemed a very long time, the head swivelled back to the pole and the chant resumed. Louie stood up. The leaves where he'd been standing were singed brown. He crouched down again and crawled with painstaking slowness through the bushes.

When he had gone a safe distance, he stood up and began to forge a trail through the wood. He was going to get Angus: Angus would know what to do. He was big and strong enough to get the mask off his cousin. Maybe he would use one of his most powerful masks to drive away this evil one. He'd be angry they had gone to the cave for the Wild Man of the Woods after he had warned them about it, but Louie would have to endure his wrath. Louie used his spear to push aside the trees. Branches whipped and stung his arms and face, but he kept on. It was slow going. Once he heard a crashing in the woods behind him. He whirled, expecting to see the Wild Man of the Woods lunge at him, but it was only a surprised deer retreating at the sound of his advance. On he went until he came to the plateau. From there he caught a glimpse of the grey lake. He heard the sound of a motorboat, felt rain on his cheek. He ran through the forest of masks, thinking how harmless these masks looked now that he had seen the Wild Man of the Woods.

Angus wasn't in the clearing. Louie lifted the teepee flap and looked inside. The old man wasn't inside there either. He called, but there was no answer. He ran back through the forest to the edge of the plateau. Behind him he heard something crash through the trees. There was a loud mumbling. The Wild Man of the Woods was coming. Louie slid down the rocky slope, stroked quickly through the sea of willows, ducked under the sentinel firs. He looked over the stormy lake. Far out he saw a green canoe. He caught sight of *The Explorer's* red nose in the green grass.

He had started towards it when a motorboat surged out of the reeds. In it were Sludge and Willard. The mumbling behind him became louder. There was a sharp crack of wood against wood as Wild Man lopped off a branch from a sentinel fir. Fearfully Louie looked over his shoulder and saw the monster mask appear from beneath the sentinel firs. It was coming straight for him.

> *Red is the fire, the fight, the fight*
> *My thirst for blood is black.*

There was no time to get into *The Explorer*. Louie threw down the knapsack and, spear in hand, leaped into the grey water.

The Wild Man of the Woods stood on the shore of the lake. Thunder reverberated inside his head. Wind blew the snaky hair across his face. Red eyes pierced the fuzzy gloom. They picked out the blurred form of someone far away paddling a green canoe. Closer to shore the eyes drilled into three boys in a motorboat. They looked vaguely familiar. One of the boys was fat, another thin. Bullies, they were the bullies he was after. He wanted to bash in their skulls. Wild Man peered at the third boy. He knew him better. He was the one he'd tied up in the cave, the one who had tried to knock off his head. He had escaped and now he had joined those bullies. This made Wild Man's bile rise hot in his mouth: he ground his teeth, slavering for revenge. *Tear away the flesh,* he rumbled. That boy had double-crossed him, which meant that he was an enemy too.

Fight! Wild Man roared at the boys in the boat. He charged forward, then remembered there was something between him and that boat. Water. Wild Man did not like water. His head turned from side to side, looking for a way to avoid touching the water and still reach those boys in the boat. His eyes lasered onto something bright red in the green grass.

He started towards the dory, swinging his sword back and forth as he went, whacking it against anything that grew in his path: trees, bushes, grass.

Break away the night, the night
Tear away the flesh.

He got into *The Explorer*, threw down his sword and shield, picked up the oars and began to row, his powerful shoulders stroking rhythmically with the chant. As he came closer to the motorboat he was pleasantly aware of helpless gestures and bulging eyes. He heard a babble of frightened voices.

"Start the motor, Sludge!"

"I can't! It's flooded."

"He's nearly here. Paddle!"

"I got nothing to paddle *with*!"

"Use your hands, then."

There was a helpless thrashing of water.

"Keep on, keep on. I'll try to hold him off with my spear."

This voice belonged to the double-crosser. Wild Man rowed towards him.

"Try the motor again!"

The motorboat rocked as a bulky weight shifted itself. Water sloshed over the bow.

"Watch it! You'll have us all overboard."

Wild Man had reached the floundering boat. He looked into the hostile, terrified eyes of a young boy. Up rose a pale arm, white as a skull-bone. It was holding a spear.

Red is the blood, the fight, the fight.

Wild Man's tongue lolled between his red lips. He grated his teeth together. He bashed his sword against the spear. The spear broke in two. One half went into the water.

Thunder rolled up the valley. It was as if the mountain dinosaurs had wakened from their prehistoric slumber transformed into fiery dragons ready for battle. Lightning fractured the sky in bone-sharp breaks. Clouds bulged low like swollen veins.

Rain splattered on Louie's head. It felt like a heavy wet blanket flapping in his face, suffocating him. Through the murky air he watched Wild Man lift his sword again.

"Paddle harder!" he screamed to the others. Willard and Sludge flailed the water with their hands. The boat jerked forward in feeble spurts.

One pull on the oars and Wild Man had caught up with them again. He dropped the oars and began thrashing the sword about in the air, his head wobbling unsteadily. For a moment Louie thought there was enough of Steve inside that terrible mask for him to recognize his cousin. Louie reached out and grabbed hold of the wooden sword blade, trying to push it into the water. He cut himself. Blood spurted across his palm. He heard the mask mouth mumble, a strange jumble of words:

Flesh . . . red . . . thirst.

Louie kept wrestling with the question of how much of his cousin was inside this creature. The creature stood up. He lifted his warrior shield and swung the sword over his ugly head.

Louie balanced what was left of his spear on his shoulder and hesitated. He wanted to destroy this evil creature, to strike it through the heart, but he still believed his cousin Steve was in that body somewhere.

Louie couldn't do it. What he did instead was to bring the spear hard against the creature's head. Wild Man of the Woods lost his balance and toppled into the lake.

The lake sizzled from the impact. There was the snarl of iron as if a blacksmith's fiery hammer had been plunged into ice water. The lake went from grey to black. It foamed and bubbled, swirled into a whirlpool. The mask didn't sink immediately. It spun in a slow circle, its mouth open, red bubbling from between shark teeth, eyes staring into the eye of the storm. There was a crash of thunder. A lightning bolt struck the whirlpool, splitting the mask in half, and it sank. The lake surface heaved and broke. Then gradually the black faded into grey.

"Hooray!" Willard and Sludge clapped their hands. "Got him!"

"Shut up, you dummies," Louie said. "You only know the half of it. My cousin's disappeared."

Louie searched the water. There was no sign of Steve. It was as if the lake had suddenly opened up and swallowed him into a deep chasm. On top of the water floated a shield, a sword and two halves of a spear.

Louie felt sick and hollow inside. Behind him Sludge and Willard lapsed into a sulky silence. Louie felt like telling them his cousin's disappearance was all their fault. *They* had *started* this war. If they hadn't been so mean, he and Steve wouldn't have been driven to getting that evil mask out of the cave and using it for revenge.

But as he sat there in tears of anger and despair, the rain falling around him, Louie knew this wasn't the whole truth. The whole truth had to include the fact that somewhere during the fighting he should have said, Stop, we won't play this game anymore. Getting even had only kept the war alive. At the time he had enjoyed it. The truthfulness of this knowledge made Louie feel worse. Through the murky air he heard the clear note of a bell. His parents were ringing for him to come home. Home was just across the lake, but it might have been in another galaxy, Louie thought. And the rain fell harder.

Stephen was several feet underwater. The blow of the mask hitting the water had stunned him. All he remembered was seeing Louie sitting in a boat with Sludge and Willard and brandishing a spear. Stephen couldn't bear to remember the look on Louie's face: it was a look of dislike and fear. Stephen sank deeper, swallowing water. He wanted the picture of Louie's hostile face to go

away. It was the face of an enemy, not a friend.
This confused him. It made him wonder if everyone in the world was his enemy. A feeling of
intense loneliness swept over him. He sank
deeper, drowning in blackness.

Then he felt himself being lifted up out of the
water.

And like a limp fish he was hauled into a green
canoe.

Twelve

Stephen lay on the chesterfield, eyes closed, listening to the murmuring sounds — low voices. The voices merged together, flowing over his head like water. Water, he remembered being underwater. The water was deep and black. He remembered lying on his back on a hard wooden surface in the rain, large hands pushing against his ribs, an open mouth breathing warm air into his. He remembered coughing up water and spewing it out. He remembered sitting up, opening his eyes and seeing that he was on the dock. Rain sprayed his face. He stared at two enormous feet bound into moccasins. His eyes travelled up a pair of long legs large as tree trunks. A pigtailed head bent forward and two huge arms picked him up.

He was carried through a storm to someplace warm. He felt tired and very sleepy. He remembered seeing the faces of his aunt and uncle. They stripped off his clothes and wrapped him in warm blankets. Then he remembered nothing. He must have fallen asleep.

Now the voices sounded more distinct. Stephen opened his eyes and turned his head. The voices were coming from the kitchen. There were other sounds, too, of logs snapping and coffee perking. Rain drummed on the roof.

Louie came in from the kitchen.

"He's awake," he called to the others.

"Louie," Stephen said. "It's you."

Louie came over to the chesterfield and sat down beside him.

"Hi, Steve," he said. "Glad you made it." His face was naked with relief and concern.

Stephen felt like crying.

Aunt Lise and Uncle Adam came into the room. Behind them Stephen saw Mrs Riley, Mr Soper, Willard and Sludge.

"Where's Angus?" was the first thing Stephen said.

"He's gone back to the woods," Aunt Lise said. "Did you know he saved your life?"

"Yes."

She put her hand on Steve's forehead. "You're still cold." Her brow wrinkled worriedly. "Would you like some soup? It's chicken rice."

"My favourite kind," Stephen said. He listened

to rain lash the trees outside. "Why did he go back?"

Uncle Adam shrugged. "We tried to get him to stay, but he wanted to go. You OK?" He looked at Stephen closely. Usually his uncle's face was relaxed, ready to break into an easy grin, but now it was drawn, deeply etched with tiredness.

"But it's stormy. Did he get across the lake all right?"

"I followed in the outboard," Mr Soper proclaimed loudly. "To make sure he got back to where he belongs."

Stephen looked at him. He noticed that Mr Soper's face was round and hard, pock-marked like a golf ball. Willard and Sludge stood beside him gaping at the inside of the log house with open curiosity. Stephen felt too weak to resent this. He felt drained and empty inside.

"Why do you say that?" Aunt Lise said sharply. She set a bowl of soup and a spoon on the table in front of Stephen.

Mr Soper took a toothpick out of his pocket and chewed on it. "Guess you folks don't know about that crazy Indian," he said.

"Now, Mel, that's no way to talk," Mrs Riley chided him. She pushed back a strand of damp hair. "He may be strange, but he's not crazy."

"What else would you call a man who wanders through the woods and paints faces on trees?" he said belligerently.

Willard smirked.

"I'll have you know those faces are masks,"
Mrs Riley replied. "Angus is a fine carver. Just
look at that!" She pointed to the sun mask.

High on the wall the giver-of-life mask glowed
softly, illuminating the cosy room.

Stephen sat up and picked up the soup. The
curved warmth of the bowl felt good in his hands.

Mel Soper barely glanced at the Sun. "Looks
like a Hallowe'en mask to me," he said, then
added, "I don't want my kid over there anyway.
Don't want him mixing with a killer."

Some of the soup slopped onto Stephen's
chest.

"What do you mean, a killer?" Louie protested.
"He fished Steve out of the lake, didn't he? He
gave him artificial respiration."

"He's the gentlest man I ever met," Stephen
said.

"Is it true that Angus killed someone?" Uncle
Adam demanded. "And if so, why were we never
told? Are we always going to be treated as
outsiders?"

Mrs Riley became agitated. Her face grew
flushed. Her hands fluttered. "Nobody is shut-
ting you out, Adam," she said. "There seemed
no point in telling you Angus had once killed
someone. Though if you remember, Lise, I did
mention to you that he'd spent some time in jail."

Stephen recalled the day when Mrs Riley had
been talking about seeing Angus on the lake and
her voice kept plunging into valleys.

"I remember."

"It was such a long time ago. And everyone can be forgiven a mistake," Mrs Riley said.

"Killing someone is hardly a mistake," Uncle Adam said.

Mrs Riley became more flustered. "I know. But my husband Bert always insisted it wasn't Angus's fault. It was when he was a hot-tempered young man, Bert said. Another young man pulled a knife on him. Bert says Angus pushed the young man away. Pushed him too hard and he fell, hit his head on a stone and died. Angus didn't know his own strength, you see. He was found guilty of manslaughter and put in jail. He was there for years and years. Bert said that's when he first began to carve."

"Putting him in jail wasn't fair," Louie said, "if it was an accident."

"Death is never fair," Mrs Riley said. She was thinking of the car crash that had killed Bert, their son and their daughter-in-law when Edward was a baby. She smoothed her dress over her round knees. "Anyway, that's all in the past. I say let bygones be bygones."

There was an awkward silence. Lise went into the kitchen and came back with a plate of ham sandwiches, which she put on the table.

"Everyone help yourselves," she said. "I'll get some coffee." She looked at Willard and Sludge. "Would you boys like some apple juice?"

They shook their heads no. Both seemed to

have been struck dumb with shyness.

Mr Soper sat down and took a sandwich.

"You heard the lady, boys. Dig in." His white teeth ripped out a slice of pink meat. He winked at Stephen and Louie. "When you're back on your feet you should get together with these guys." He jerked a thumb at Willard and Sludge. "Maybe they'll let you have a spin on their motor-bikes. Give you some thrills."

Stephen looked into his empty soup bowl. That'll be the day, he thought.

Louie bit his lip to keep from saying he'd had enough thrills to last him the summer.

Mel Soper gulped down his coffee and stood up. "Got to get back to the wife," he said. "She'll be fretting about us. Won't do her ticker any good. Let's go, boys." He paused in front of Mrs Riley. "You want a lift, Ardelle? If we all hold our breaths we can squeeze into the cab." He grinned and slapped Mrs Riley on the back.

Willard snickered, but Sludge shuffled his feet uncomfortably.

"Thank you, Mel," Mrs Riley said demurely.

Aunt Lise and Uncle Adam followed their visitors to the door.

"Were your parents mad at us for staying over there in the storm?" Stephen said.

"They were too worried to be mad."

"Did you tell them about . . ." he paused, then went on quickly, "about the mask?"

"Nah," Louie said. "I told them it was a boat accident. I didn't want to tell them about all those dumb things we did." He grinned. "Maybe when they're old enough, I'll tell them. After they've grown up."

Stephen smiled wanly.

"What were . . . ?" He stopped. He found it difficult to remember that Louie had been in Riley's motorboat with Willard and Sludge. "What were those guys doing out on the lake in a storm?"

"They were looking for the paddle they dropped. I guess they used it when they were sneaking up on us the night before."

"What about Angus? Why was he there?"

Louie shrugged. "Who knows? Maybe he was trying on his wind mask again, though I didn't see it on."

"If he did, it sure worked," Stephen said. He closed his eyes, remembering the wind whipping up waves on the lake.

There was a long pause.

Then Louie asked a question that had been bugging him ever since they had fished Steve out of the lake.

"Were you really going to hurt me with that sword?" he said. "I was real scared."

"Nah. I would never hurt you." Stephen gave Louie a shove.

Louie shoved him back, but not too hard. Steve still looked shaky.

"Are you scared of Angus?" he said. "I mean, now that you know about him killing someone? I know it was an accident and he told us about it and everything, but . . ." His voice trailed away.

"Nah, I'm not afraid of him," Stephen said, "or Willard or Sludge."

He could have added Terry Mulcaster.

He wasn't afraid of bullies anymore. He felt that that weight had been lifted from his shoulders. Still, he felt tired. It was as if one weight had been removed, only to be replaced by another, heavier burden.

"I guess," he said wearily, "what scares me most is myself."

He sank back into the pillows and closed his eyes.

The storm continued. During the night the wind swept on stage. Disguised in darkness it shrieked and wailed, then moaned in corners of the loft like a dying ventriloquist. Neither Stephen nor Louie heard this performance; both slept on, camped deep in dreams.

By morning the wind had exhausted itself, but the rain continued.

It rained for three days.

The first day Louie wandered about the house fretting about his pup tent, which would be drenched by now. Even the sleeping bags would be soaked through. He picked up Risk, intending to ask Steve if he felt like a game, but his cousin was asleep. He didn't really want to play anyway. He was tired of the game. He threw it into a box along with his toy soldiers and kicked it under his bunk. Then he went downstairs to help his father in the workshop.

Stephen spent most of the three days in bed. Sometimes he picked up *Great Masks* and leafed through it. He came to the picture of the death mask, where a man's whole lifetime was written on his face. *Give a man a mask and he will tell the truth.* Again he wondered what that meant, what the truth was. Could wearing a mask make you tell the truth about yourself, things like violence and revenge that you'd rather hide in nightmares? Is that what those cruel pictures were all about? Was the truth that meanness wasn't just in the faces of other people but in your own as well, where you couldn't see it? It was this thought, that he was no better than the people who'd been bullying him, that depressed Stephen most of all. He wasn't ready to face this. It was a lot easier to stay in bed and feel sorry for himself.

He didn't dare look at the picture of the Wild Man of the Woods. He never wanted to see that face again. He wondered if the mask was at the bottom of the lake or whether it had moved. Louie had said the lake was fed by underground streams. What if the mask had fallen into one of those streams? Would it travel elsewhere? Would it appear someday in some other place? Or would it lurk down there forever, prowling around on the bottom like an ugly lake monster? Stephen looked out the window at the lake, but it gave nothing away. It was merely a darker shape behind a screen of lighter grey rain. Even the mountain was nothing more than a blurred shadow.

On the fourth day the sun finally appeared, its long rays reaching tentatively into the loft in first morning, wakening the Barrows.

Louie bounded out of bed.

"C'mon, Steve," he thumped his cousin's sleeping body. "Get up. The sun's out." Stephen groaned in his sleep. Louie dressed quickly and went downstairs. His mother was making a big pot of oatmeal; his father was frying bacon.

"After we eat I'm going into the village for groceries and the mail," Uncle Adam said. "Want to come?"

"Might as well," Louie said glumly. "Steve's still in bed."

"Maybe he'll be up by the time you get back," his mother said, but she sounded doubtful.

When they returned two hours later with four bags of food and the mail, Stephen was still in bed.

"How can he sleep so much?" Louie said disgustedly. He made no effort to keep his voice down.

Adam poured himself a cup of coffee and sat

down to sort the mail. Lise began unpacking the groceries.

"You know, I'm beginning to wonder if there's something seriously wrong with Stephen," she said thoughtfully. "Since the boat accident he hasn't seemed at all well. I'm worried about him. Perhaps we should call Louise. He may need to see a specialist in the city."

Upstairs Stephen lifted his head from the pillow and listened.

"Maybe he's homesick," he heard his uncle say. "He's been here two weeks. A month might be too long for him. Maybe we should ask him if he'd like to go home."

"I feel guilty that we haven't spent more time with him," Aunt Lise said. "But with the craft fair and the shop to keep up . . ." Her voice trailed away.

Stephen heard Uncle Adam's voice again. "Louie, take this postcard up to your cousin. Maybe it'll cheer him up."

Louie took the postcard upstairs. Stephen was already sitting up in bed. He took the card. It was from his father in Greece. On the front was a picture of a temple at night. White columns were lit up against a black sky. They looked like gods and goddesses holding back the dark. There was something triumphant and eternal about the picture. On the back his father had written in his precise handwriting:

Tour going well. Engine trouble crossing from Naxos but otherwise no major problems. It's hot as Hades. I envy you the cool nights. Enjoy yourself.

Love, Dad

Stephen looked at the picture again and reread the message. *Enjoy yourself,* it said. He looked at the sun on the green blanket. It made a wavy pattern as the trees outside moved slightly in the breeze. He thought of the cove, the lime-coloured water dappled in sunlight. He looked at the blue sky: not a cloud anywhere. He couldn't get out of bed fast enough. There were so many things here to enjoy and he had barely begun.

"C'mon, Louie, we'd better get going," he said. He rummaged through the jumble of clothes on the floor looking for his swim-suit. He put it on.

"Let's go swimming. We've got to go over to the other side of the lake. Got to get the tent and stuff. Got to thank Angus for fishing me out of the lake. Got to salvage more junk out of the lake." He pulled on his Stampede City shirt. "I've only got two more weeks before I go home, you know." He shoved his feet into his soiled Nikes and went downstairs. "What's there to eat?" he said. "I'm starving."

Thirteen

Stephen stood at their campsite and watched his cousin crawl out of the pup tent.

"It's nearly dry except for the floor," Louie said. "But the sleeping bags are still damp and the mattresses are soaked."

"Let's leave them to dry while we go up and see Angus," Stephen said. They spread the bedding on the grass in the sun. Neither of them noticed that the green canoe was gone.

They ducked beneath the sentinel firs, waded through the sea of willows and climbed the rocky embankment to the plateau. Above them the mountain rose silent as a sealed tomb.

As they walked into the forest of masks Stephen felt the eyes of the broken-nosed great world rim being staring at him. But the divided face no longer seemed ugly. Today the eyes were kind and friendly. He stroked the coarse straw hair and twirled the mask lightly on its rope. Overhead the trees sighed and whispered, rocking comfortably in the breeze. Beneath, in the lower branches, were the familiar faces of Bear and Coyote and full-cheeked Wind. The masks gleamed softly in the sunlight, bright and luminous. Stephen felt that if he were to lie in the centre of the courtyard and shut his eyes, the colours of the masks would whirl inside his head like spinning tops. He lay down on the needled floor, Louie beside him, their heads pillowed on Crooked Beak's belly.

The peacefulness of the woods overtook them. Stephen thought the whole wilderness, and all the forests of the past, had been tamed.

But Louie thought of a different wilderness. He thought of other galaxies, of snowball comets streaking through darkness, their dust particles reflecting light. He thought of moons shining coldly in the night sky.

"I wonder," he said. "If we put people into outer space will we carry war out there too?" He added, "Like garbage?"

"There must be someplace that isn't contaminated," Stephen said. He meant a place that was perfect—for him, peace was more than an absence of war.

"Maybe it's here," Louie said.

They lay in the sun, savouring it. The peace

and the light, clear air made them feel happy. After a while Louie shielded his eyes and looked at the flaming circle of fire. It was directly overhead.

"It's noon," he said. "I guess we've got to get going." They continued through the forest of uncarved trees until they came to Angus's clearing. Here they felt their happiness sliding away. It was as if the mountain had suddenly shifted beneath their feet. The clearing was empty. There was no teepee, no stool, no work-bench, tools or paints, no Angus. The circle was so empty that for a moment they wondered if Angus had really been here.

"Where did he go?" Louie said.

"Maybe he went to sell some of his masks."

"Nah. He wouldn't take his teepee with him just to do that," Louie said. "Besides, he left his masks here. We saw them, didn't we?"

They had to walk back through the forest of masks to make sure. There were the half human, half animal faces with their distorted smiles grinning at them as if they knew where Angus had gone but would never tell.

"Remember what Mrs Riley said about Angus disappearing—that he always came back?" Stephen said, but it wasn't much help.

Disconsolate, they walked back to the campsite. They worked in silence, taking down the tent and folding it, stowing the sleeping bags and mattresses in the dory.

"He took his canoe," Louie said.

Both of them felt betrayed, as if Angus had abandoned them like newborn babies on a doorstep. But neither of them said this. Instead Louie surveyed *The Explorer* critically. "We'll have to get this bucket fixed up before my sister comes home. If she sees it like this she'll be cross. And when Mad is mad, she's *really* mad."

They got into the dory and Louie rowed. The boat creaked arthritically. "All that damp," Louie said.

Stephen stared into the green water. Trout darted through the jungle of magical trees, their shapes sleek as submarines. There was no sign of the beaver.

"I wonder where the beaver is?" he said. "It's like he's extinct. Do you think Mr Soper trapped him?"

"Nah," Louie said. "He never plugged up the culvert this year."

They sat on the beaver lodge and looked at the still water. A trout splashed in front of them. Rings of water spread outward into folds of liquid glass.

"Maybe the beaver and Angus went to another lake farther into the wilderness," Louie said.

He got back into the dory.

Stephen looked at the deep part of the lake where the water was darkest, a monster's lair. Then his eyes swept up the mountainside to the cave impaled on the tree-top like a pierced eye.

"I wonder why he didn't destroy the Wild Man of the Woods?" he said, "knowing it was so evil."

"He told us, people were afraid of it, remember?" Louie said slowly. "I suppose in a way it's like weapons."

"Weapons?"

"Yeah, bombs and stuff." Louie groped for the words. "Maybe something terrible has got to be there to scare us into our senses."

Stephen thought for a while. "I'm not sure that's true," he said.

Louie picked up the oars. "Get in," he said.

They rowed across the lake. The mother duck paddled past them, six furry babies enclosed in the V of her wake.

Behind them the sun exploded on the cave entrance, obliterating it with light.

They reached the raft and climbed out of the boat. Louie tied up *The Explorer*. They peeled off their clothes. Stephen was first into the water, which was cool after the rain. They swam out to the cove entrance and back. Stephen put on the mask and flippers and snorkelled over to the footprints. They were still there, though fainter now: soon they would be gone. He swam back to the raft. Louie was sunning himself on a towel.

"Those footprints were Angus's all right," Stephen said. "He must've come swimming over here."

"I've never seen him swimming," Louie said.

Stephen hauled himself out of the lake and took

off his snorkelling equipment. He lay down beside Louie and closed his eyes.

"He must've done it at night," he said. He imagined Angus lying in the moonlit water. To a giant the cove would seem like a bathtub.

"Hey, you guys," a voice called. "Come over here for a minute."

It was Willard and Sludge. They were standing on the Barrows' dock in their bathing suits.

Stephen looked at Louie. Neither boy lifted his head.

"Think we should go?" Louie said.

"It might be a trap."

Louie sat up.

"What do you want?" he yelled.

"Want to show you something," Sludge yelled back.

Louie and Stephen got into *The Explorer* and made the long journey back to the dock. They climbed out of the dory.

"It's over here," Sludge said. In his bathing suit he looked like a shorn sheep. And Willard looked as if he'd been plucked of feathers: his ribs showed through, and he had knobby knees.

Sludge passed the salvage bin and went into the bushes. The others followed. Stephen still suspected an ambush. They mounted the ladder to the tree-lab and climbed in through the door.

The four of them crowded into the tiny room. Louie saw that the floor had been swept free of glass. The shelves had been tidied. The dummy was gone. There were half a dozen pickle jars on the shelves. They were none too clean, and there were no specimens, but at least people could stand on the floor in their bare feet and not cut themselves.

He was too astonished to speak.

Finally he said, "Well thanks, you guys." Then to cover his embarrassment he shouted, "Let's go for a swim."

He backed down the ladder and wrenched the NO TRESPASSING sign free of its nails. Later he used it, along with the broken spear, the sword and the shield, to make a bonfire.

Forgiveness did not come as easily to Stephen. He followed the others to the dock. They unloaded the camping gear. The four of them crowded into *The Explorer*. With the extra weight, mostly Sludge's, it took longer to get to the raft, but no one said anything.

As soon as they had tied up and Stephen was climbing out of the dory, Willard gave him a shove. Stephen fell backwards into the water. He went under, then came up laughing. He hoisted himself onto the raft and gave Willard a big push. Willard disappeared into the blue-green water. When he came up he was coughing and gasping for breath.

"I can't swim!" he yelled. There was fear in his face.

This made it easier. Stephen put out a hand and pulled him in.

"I'll teach you," he said. He felt good and strong saying this. He gave Willard another push, then fished him out again.

"And I'll teach you," Louie said. "First lesson." He gave Sludge a shove.

Sludge went under and immediately bobbed back up.

"For a fat person, you're buoyant," Louie said admiringly, "really buoyant. Floating'll be easy for you."

It took longer for Willard.

After they had practised swimming, they lay on the raft. The sun gilded their bodies in shining light. Stephen looked into the lake of glass. He squinched up his eyes and stuck out his tongue, then laughed at his comic reflection, at the greatest mask-maker of them all.

Aunt Lise brought peanut butter sandwiches and Kool-Aid to the dock. Sludge went home and came back with a chocolate cake. They sat on the dock and ate their lunch, listening to the red-winged blackbird warning them about her nest in the reeds. The campground was silent. From across the lake came the haunting call of the loon.

"My grandma can imitate that," Sludge said proudly. "She knows all the bird calls."

After they had eaten, they lay back to rest their stomachs and closed their eyes against the sun's brilliance. Stephen put on his Stampede City shirt so he wouldn't burn. Then they went swimming again.

They swam until the sun went down, until their part of the earth had spun itself into shade. Still they felt its gentle power. Leaping and splashing, their smooth bodies were like salmon travelling upriver to spawn. They swam with a frantic kind of gaiety, as if they knew time was as fragile as glass. As if they knew this imperfect peace, this truce, had been hard to find. *And must be held.*